Ernest and Newell
The Brothers

Warmest wishes,
Kathy Ferrara

Kathleen Ferrara

Ernest and Newell: The Brothers is a work of fiction. Any similarity regarding names, characters, settings, or incidents is entirely coincidental.

Copyright© 2022 by Katheen Ferrara

Published in the United States

Paperback ISBN: 978-1-951854-32-4

Dedication

This book is dedicated, posthumously, to my beloved husband Jim, who passed away in November of 2021 after a truly courageous nine-year battle against a rare cancer.

He would have been beyond happy and extremely proud that I completed this after such a long hiatus, and it is ironic that it came into fruition only because of his passing.

Rest in peace, My Love.

Introduction

This book was nearly thirty years in the making. A cross-country train trip: A writer's workshop called Trains of Thought in 1993, and a simple assignment to write a story based on one line written by a fellow writer, was the beginning of this journey. Thank you to the Leader of the Pack, Charlie Hunter, for your line that inspired these stories. I wrote "Sprint" and "Millie's Place" on the trip, wrote two more chapters later that year, and then put them aside.

Fast forward to 2014. While taking Tai Chi classes at a yoga center, I met Jerry Lagadec, a former English professor and an author himself. I asked if he would read those four stories I had written so long ago. He gave me a very positive critique and enthusiastically encouraged me to get back to writing, turn the stories into a book, and get it published.

But life got in the way.

My husband had been diagnosed in 2012 with an incurable and debilitating cancer, and my life was dedicated to taking care of him until he finally passed in 2021. I am an artist by profession, but I retired my brushes. I had no motivation to paint or to write. After he passed, I was drowning in overwhelming grief, and, as a distraction, I began writing again, so driven that I wrote a chapter a day for eighteen days straight. I barely slept. It was as though these two brothers had to tell me their story and all I could do was sit back and listen, taking notes along the way. Even when I thought the book was finished, the chapters kept coming. It had a life of its own. It was in control, and I was, seemingly, just an observer of the process.

I am truly grateful to my friends Linda Killion, Peter Swanson, Leo MacNeil, and my Hospice counselor, Rosemary MacKay, for their patience in listening to and reading the chapters as they unfolded, encouraging me every step of the way. And to Virginia Young, a friend and talented artist and author, who was charmed by the brothers' tale, and helped me find my publisher.

Ironically, I was in my forties when this all began, and the older folks who read the stories would ask – "You're so young. How do you know what old people are thinking?"

Well, now that I have several more decades under my belt, I see that I really did know what many "old" people are thinking. I guess I'm just an Old Soul. There is a lot of Newell in me, (or is it the other way around?)

Their Stories

Do not go gentle into that good night,
Old age should burn and rave at close of day;
Rage, rage against the dying of the light.

Dylan Thomas

Sprint

The brothers make their slow way across the wet cemetery lawn, Newell's painful step-wait, step-wait movement allowing no speed, no stride. Ernest, six years his junior, walks along beside him, Newell holding his arm for support.

Rainy days were tough on Newell. His gnarly arthritic hands swelling, pulsing with hurt when the lows hit. On sunny days he'd get angry, mumbling, "Damn," under his breath when he saw the sun-burned, sandlot-ball kids running, diving, tearing around the bases.

Last August, he scared the wits out of Ernest, bolting from a near standstill at Main and Carlton, right into the street. Made it almost halfway, tilting, head jutting forward, fists clenched, until he wobbled a bit, then swayed, staggering, and keeled over, flat on his back, and just laid there.

He wasn't hurt, just mad. Got it into his head that he'd run across the street to the other side. Newell Madison, 79, who hadn't stood without support of some kind in three years.

If Newell was mad, Ernest was even madder, fit to be tied once he found out that Newell wasn't dead, just lying there – mad.

Traffic was making a natural path around them and the crowd that had gathered to help or just stare. Once they got him back up on the sidewalk and dusted off, Ernest read him the riot act.

And Newell spit on him.

Pulled up as much moisture as an old man's mouth can manage and blew it, hard as he could, at Ernest's feet. Feet that represented all that Newell didn't have – Mobility. Independence. Freedom.

Today, as they make their way back to the car, the sky opens slightly, and Ernest absentmindedly lets the umbrella fall back, exposing their old heads to the warm spring rain, neither one noticing.

They never talk about that day last summer, and Ernest still drives his brother to Glenvale twice a month and stands there quietly while Newell pays his respects to Catherine, who waits.

The days go on, one right after the other, and Newell hasn't tried running again. Not since Ernest chewed him out.

Millie's Place

"Pay attention, dammit," Newell snapped, as Ernest led him into the door jamb for the fourth time this month. It wasn't that they liked each other's company much, but the twice a week lunch at Millie's was a welcome break from the monotony of their tired lives. Once in a while, they would go to one of the Italian places downtown, just to change things up, but Millie's was comfortable, like an old pair of shoes.

The restaurant was a favorite with the locals, its faded red and white gingham café curtains giving the place a warm inviting glow. Breakfast, served all day, was a real draw. Aromas of good coffee being brewed, bacon sizzling on the flat-top, and cinnamon, filled the air.

Ernest always ordered the same thing: Chicken salad on white, hold the pickle. Orange Crush. Coffee-light after, with a big oozy slice of Millie's peach pie.

Newell made a point of ordering something different every time they came in. Gracie would try to guess his order, but never got it right.

"Ham on rye today, Sugar?" she'd ask, bending in close as if he couldn't hear her, the discount-store cologne she wore annoying his nose.

"Ham and *Swiss* on rye!" he'd yell in her ear, squinting, his gray-blue eyes barely visible through the slits.

Once, two years ago, before she knew better, Gracie brought out Newell's grilled cheese and tomato sandwich with the crusts cut off.

"Here you go, Sweetie," she said, smiling, placing it in front of him on her way to the next booth.

"Missy! Hey, Missy!" he shouted, louder to his ears than hers. She turned back to him as he slid the plate to the edge of the table. "Run this through the blender for me, will you, Honey?"

Gracie burst into bosomy laughter that started at her feet and worked its way up, but stopped when she saw that Newell wasn't smiling. Glaring at her, he said it again, slowly this time.

"Put my sandwich in the blender…please."

Gracie had worked at Millie's Place for six and a half years and at The Sunny Egg before that, so she'd seen it all, she figured, until now. She took Newell's sandwich back to the kitchen, shaking her head.

Ernest, now halfway through his lunch, said in a low angry tone, "What the hell are you pulling now, Newell? Can't you, for once, just EAT?"

This was met with silence.

Gracie brought the sandwich back in a bowl. She didn't know if he wanted it heated up, so she put it in the microwave for a minute, just in case. Brought along a spoon, too. She put the bowl down in front of him and studied the old face for a reaction. Ernest was watching him, too. Newell dipped the spoon into the liquid sandwich and brought it slowly, shakily, up to his mouth, spilling a bit along the way. He took a hard swallow and looked up at Gracie who was standing there as if glued to the spot.

"Delicious. Now, tell Millie to put this on the menu for old people like me who can't chew the crusts of their bread."

Gracie got a hurt look on her face, placed their check on the table and backed away, turning to another customer.

"For Pete's sake, Newell, she was just trying to be helpful," Ernest said as he put a few bills and change on the table under the check.

"If I embarrass you, Ernest, then we can just quit coming here, just stay home is all," Newell said as Ernest helped him up from the well-worn red leatherette seat.

As they neared the exit, Gracie forced a smile and yelled, competing with the radio, "So long, boys! Come back again!"

"So long, Gracie!" Ernest replied, turning to wave.

Nothing out of Newell. He was heading for the door jamb, banking hard left.

Instinct

The cat just showed up one day, mewing at the side door, scrawny, unfed – a pitiful-looking gray tabby cat with a black stripe down its back, no telling its age. It got into the house by accident when Ernest was helping Newell through the screen door. It just scooted by and watched them from near the refrigerator until they got in.

"Shoo, Cat!" Ernest yelled, making shooing gestures at the forlorn animal, chasing it from room to room. As they made their way around the first floor, Newell was pouring a bowl of milk and setting it on the kitchen floor, spilling a bit on the way down.

As Ernest was yelling, "Scoot, cat! scoot!," Newell was calling, "Here kitty, kitty! Here, puss!"

The cat barreled around the corner with Ernest in hot pursuit and slid to a halt when it spotted the milk. Ernest almost smacked right into Newell as he came striding breathlessly around the corner after the cat.

"Newell, what are you doing?! Now we'll never get rid of it!" Ernest moaned, as the happy cat slurped up the welcome milk.

They named it Max. That was before a trip to the vet to determine if it was spayed and up to date on its shots. By the time they learned that Max was a female, the name had stuck, and so be it.

Max knew Ernest didn't like her, and, in a cat kind of way,

tormented him daily.

As many times as Ernest would sweep her off the kitchen counter, Max would take up residence there whenever he was in the room, nonchalantly licking her paws. He bought her a scratching post, but Max preferred to disembowel his easy chair, leaving little tufts of stuffing all over the braided rug. At night, Ernest would sleep on his back, snoring a good part of the time, and every morning he would awaken to the sight of Max, sitting Sphinx-like on his chest, staring at him, purring. And every time he would relax into his chair, the cat jumped up on his lap, circling several times to find just the right spot, then would knead his legs with her front paws, occasionally digging in with her claws, then fall asleep. It drove him nuts.

Newell and Max were pals. He would slip some tuna fish, smuggled from the market, into her cat food, affectionately rub her chin, neck, and ears, and he kept a supply of catnip on hand, just to enjoy her drunken antics. Every night, when Newell had his dish of vanilla ice cream, Max would enjoy a dish, too. As time went on, and Newell's legs continued to fail him, Max was a real comfort. Most days Ernest and Newell would just grate on each other, and Max was a kind of salve. She was a good listener.

One day, on the way back to the car at the cemetery, the brothers spotted an injured bird under a bush. It couldn't fly and fell over as it tried to hop away.

Newell said, "Ernest, get that bird, he's hurt."

"Newell, I have enough with trying to get *you* home, much less a half-dead bird."

"Then take me home and come back for it," Newell said, angrily. "And be quick about it, before a cat gets him."

Ernest really did not want to become involved with this bird's problems, but deep down he knew it was the right thing to do. He took

Newell home, got a shoebox out of the closet, punched a couple of holes in the top, and left to retrieve the bird, hoping it would be gone by the time he got back. To his dismay, it was still there, a few inches from where they had spotted it.

Ernest set up a cardboard box near the window in the pantry and put shredded newspaper and a bowl of water on the bottom. He attached a piece of chicken wire over the top, securing it with a couple of staples. In went the bird, and the pantry door was closed. Max was extremely interested in this new turn of events, but, naturally, she was barred from the area.

For three weeks they nurtured the bird, feeding it ground sunflower seeds and water from an eyedropper, Ernest grumbling all the while. A couple of times it looked like they'd lost him. He'd be lying lifeless in the box, just staring wide-eyed. But, with a gentle poke, he'd come around, and the vigil continued.

Finally, the bird showed signs of healthy activity – recuperation. They chose a day for release with great anticipation. (The house had taken on a sick-bird smell). As much as Ernest had complained, he found himself feeling a twinge of pride for having saved the life of a distressed creature, even though it was just a homely starling, not one of his favorite birds.

It was a fine spring day. Ernest took the box out to the porch, propped the screen door open with it, and went back in for Newell. He got him settled in a lawn chair and went back for the box. The bird was flapping wildly, so he took care when removing the chicken wire. He reached in and gently picked it up in both hands, held it for a brief moment, then flung it in the air. The bird flapped its wings a bit, faltered, then plopped to the ground, hopping and peeping.

Ernest quickly approached it and picked it up again. The bird didn't seem injured, and Newell shouted, "Go!" He tried it again. The bird flew in a deep arc then fluttered slowly down to earth again, landing softly on the grass.

From under a bush, Max shot out like a bullet, and, in a flash, the bird and Max were gone. She had gotten out when the door was held open and had patiently watched the proceedings.

Newell and Ernest were speechless. They stayed in the yard for a while, staring at the spot where the bird had disappeared. Finally, Ernest helped Newell up the stairs and into the house. Max came home about an hour later.

That night, Ernest and Newell played cards.

Max didn't get any ice cream.

And Ernest and Newell, simply because they didn't like to re-hash bad memories, never mentioned the bird again.

The Shopping Trip

They never agreed on much, especially the kind of cereal, or TV dinners, or deli meats to buy, so making up the shopping list was always a chore. Once a week, they went to the A&P. Ernest would have preferred to go alone, but Newell insisted on joining him. It was pushing the shopping cart he liked the best. He could hang onto it and walk along, this being the only time out of the whole week that he didn't have to hang onto a cane, or a walker, or Ernest for support.

This excursion was typical: At the deli counter, Ernest took a number and waited next to Newell, both of them surveying the choices. When the girl behind the counter said, "Number seventeen, please," both of them spoke up:

"Half a pound of roast beef, rare."

"Half a pound of olive pimento loaf."

She gave them a puzzled look and said, "Which would you like, gentlemen?"

They didn't hear her. They were too busy arguing about which cold cuts to get. Neither one would budge, so Ernest finally said, "Half a pound of boiled ham, sliced thin."

This is the way it would go throughout the whole store. Ernest took Cream of Wheat off the shelf as Newell reached for a box of Rice Krispies. They couldn't afford both, and there was no compromising, so they put both cereals back, and Ernest threw a box of Frosted Flakes into the cart with an angry snort.

They were grousing at each other at the frozen food case when Newell spotted Gert Stimpson passing the end of the aisle, heading toward Dairy at the far end of the store. "Damn," he said under his breath.

Gert had a crush on him in junior high and apparently never got over it. Once Catherine died, she had made a point of dropping by the house armed with baked goodies: gingerbread, hermits, pumpkin and zucchini breads, all dust-dry and spiced too highly with nutmeg and cloves. He stopped answering the door after a while, and she finally gave up, but she latched onto him every time they met at the market.

Newell hated to leave Ernest with the decision on the TV dinners, (he hated Salisbury Steak), but he headed the cart in the direction she had just come from, looking to avoid her at all costs. He cursed his inability to hurry, moving as fast as his wobbly legs would carry him, which wasn't very fast at all.

Gert had that kind of short-cropped, tightly curled haircut that old ladies got, with a bluish-purple cast to it. Why women thought that blue hair was attractive, Newell could never figure out.

He got all the way to the canned seafood aisle and had just hidden a can of tuna under the Wonder Bread in the cart when he heard...

"Newell! Hello, Dear! It's so nice to run into you!" He knew he was in for a good fifteen minutes of conversation, mostly hers, and felt a little panicky at the lack of an escape route.

"I just saw Ernest a few aisles over, and he said you were down here. I'm so glad I found you! Say, did I tell you about my bout with the flu? I was down for days! My goodness, the cough was..."

"*What*? Whatcha say?" Newell said, leaning toward her as if straining to hear.

"I said my FLU, Newell. I had the flu something terrible, and then my back went out, and my hot water bottle leaked all over the sofa, and, oh, Dot Parsons called and told me about Madge and Howard's bad luck, and…"

"What?! Can't hear you!" he said, quite loudly.

She stopped talking and just looked at him, unsure of what to do next. Finally, she shouted, "Well, I'll be seeing you, Newell!" so loud that the whole store probably heard her, and went down the aisle with her cart, and her blue hair, and around the endcap and out of sight.

Wearing a satisfied grin, he headed back and found Ernest, whose arms were loaded with chicken pot pies, frozen mixed vegetables, a quart of vanilla ice cream, and a few boxes of TV dinners. Newell was tilting his head, trying to read the labels when Ernest yelled…

"Newell, my hands are freezing! I need the cart! Where the heck have you been?!"

"Oh, just chatting with Gert Stimpson. Thanks for telling her where to find me," he said, squinting angrily.

After another argument in the paper goods aisle, they stood in line at the checkout.

They got Holly this time. She was short, had a ruddy round face, and her frizzy auburn hair was pulled back in a ponytail. She was soft-spoken and quite shy, but she always warmed up and relaxed with the older customers.

Newell's legs were really tired. He was pushing it, being on his feet for so long, but these shopping trips, as aggravating as they were, were something he refused to give up.

He distracted Ernest at the candy bars long enough for the tuna to be checked through and bagged. He'd get a talking-to when they got home, but by then it would be too late. Max would have her treat again this week.

"I feel like a Snickers, today," Newell said, fingering the brown and blue candy wrapper, and picturing the delicious sensation of chocolate, caramel, and nuts on his old tongue.

"You know you're not supposed to have nuts, Newell. Here, have a Three Musketeers instead," Ernest said, picking up the bar and holding it out to his brother.

Newell gave him a *look* and put the Snickers back on the shelf. He took the Three Musketeers from Ernest, and put it back as well. Ernest paid Holly, and told Newell to wait on the bench while he put the groceries in the car.

Today there was no one else in line, so Holly told Ernest to go on ahead, she would help Newell over to the seat, and when she did, she slipped a Snickers into his jacket pocket. He found it as soon as he got home, smiled, and his mouth watered at the thought of this sweet delight that he would savor at bedtime, after Ernest turned in.

He sat at the kitchen table while Ernest emptied the grocery bags and put the food and dry goods away. As expected, when he came across the Chicken of the Sea, Ernest lectured Newell on how tight their budget was, how high the cost of tuna was, and on and on.

Newell just sat there and listened, just waiting to see what kind of TV dinners Ernest pulled out of the bag.

Typos

When Newell was seventeen, he dropped out of school and got a job as a gopher at a small advertising agency in town. The boys' father had suffered a work-related injury and was unable to continue full-time, so Newell felt compelled to help the family in whatever small way he could. He had his learner's permit to drive and was excited and proud. First, about his new job, and second, to be able to get behind the wheel of his dad's car, all by himself.

The Wright Idea was owned by cousins Adam and Joel Wright, and their contracts included several local businesses, including Hoffman's Department Store, Carroll's Clothiers, Leaf and Lawn Garden Center, and Lincoln Appliance. The company was well thought of in the area and known to be fair in its business practices.

A gopher was an entry-level position. The term stood for 'go-for.' Newell's tasks included picking up ad information from various clients; getting coffee for the advertising manager and the staff in the art department; changing the ink in the copiers; making sure the paper trays were full, and numerous other simple jobs. He was fascinated by the whole process of print advertising. On his breaks, he would ask permission to watch the various art department staff as they did their jobs – illustrators, paste-up people, layout artists, and the camera room operators. He was a sponge – soaking up every bit of what he observed. He came to learn the names and use of all the tools of the trade: Triangles and long metal T-Squares, plastic ellipses, kneaded erasers, X-Acto blades, register marks printed on rolls of clear tape, smallnibbed Rapidograph pens used for touching up copy and art, acetate overlays for color separation, rubber cement, transfer paper, and vellum. A myriad of materials and implements, all of it interesting and giving him a thirst for more.

Adam and Joel were impressed by his enthusiasm, and, before long, Newell was promoted to Paste-Up. In their office, after discussing his salary, Adam said, sternly, "Attention to *detail*, Newell. Your vision: PRECISION!"

"Yes, sir! I will make you proud," he replied, feeling confident in his words.

The process went like this: A client would present the agency with products that were to be featured in the following week's newspaper ad or flyer. That information would go to the layout person, who would format the page as it would appear in print. The layout then went to Harriet, the copywriter, who used her writing talents to make such simple items like shovels, toasters, hairspray, and Bermuda shorts sound like they were something one simply *must* have. The illustrators and fashion artists would draw accurate pictures of the sale products, and they would be brought to the camera room for sizing to fit the layouts. The body copy was printed out on long sheets of white paper, then brought to the paste-up person, who would apply adhesive to the back of it by carefully running it through an electric waxer. Then, using the layout as his guide, he would carefully cut out the waxed pieces of copy with a razor-sharp X-Acto blade and paste them onto a clean white board, leaving the designated space for an illustration or a photograph. Newell would true it up, using the T-square and triangle, always keeping in mind Adam's admonition to be precise.

Every line of copy had to be arrow-straight and perpendicular to both edges of the board. Product illustrations and/or photographs would be adhered to the board in the predetermined areas of the layout. The finished product would be sent back to the copywriter for proof-reading, and then sent off to be printed.

Newell had a great eye for this work. He quickly learned how to make all the copy perfectly level, and he had a real knack for finding typos, which were either misspellings or improper sentence structure. He had gotten in the habit of reading all the text before he let the boards out of his hands, and, more often than not, he would spot a spelling error.

At first, not wanting to ruffle any feathers, he let them go through, but after a few times watching Paul, the Art Director, yelling at the top of his lungs about the sloppiness of the work and threatening to have Harriet fired, Newell decided to speak to her privately, because once the proofs went out, there was no correcting anything. It was too late, it was "Put to bed," and the newspaper ad or flyer would go to press.

He gingerly knocked on the door of Harriet's office, went up to her desk, and asked if it was okay to alert her if he noticed a mistake in her copy. He said he would subtly make her aware of it and she could re-type the copy and drop it off at his drafting table. It would be their little secret. She gratefully agreed, knowing that her job would be saved, and she truly appreciated his having her back.

"What a nice young man!" she said, when he left her office.

As much as he enjoyed working in the office, he really liked his appointments with the clients. It got him outside in the fresh air, driving Dad's Chevy, and, on one of these trips, he happened to meet a sweet girl who worked at Hoffman's – Catherine, with whom he would spend the very best years of his life.

Newell eventually became Assistant Art Director. On the whole, it was a satisfying career and he made a good living at it. He remained at *The Wright Idea* until retiring at sixty-seven years of age.

But…there was one downside to his career in advertising. Not for

Newell, but for Ernest. Now, every time they went somewhere, be it an office, a restaurant, or the barber shop, Newell would either find a typo on a menu, or notice a crooked picture on the wall.

"Ernest, go straighten that picture over there."

"Ernest, go grab the manager and tell him there's a typo in this menu."

"You're like a damn Border Collie, Newell! Just leave it alone, will you?!" he'd say, knowing full well that he wouldn't.

"Attention to detail, Ernest. Attention to detail."

Once you developed an eye for these things, you never lost it. Newell was a well-trained sheep dog.

Some Tears are Good Tears

There wasn't much in the way of laughter in the house. Occasionally Max would perform some comical acrobatics after consuming a little catnip, resulting in some brief chuckles from the brothers, but smiles were few and far between.

One morning, Newell was sitting at the kitchen table, reading the newspaper and enjoying the spring bird songs through the open window when he heard Ernest cursing from the bathroom. He had banged his shin on the toilet. Shortly, he blew into the kitchen, without even a "Good morning," and proceeded to pour himself a bowl of cereal and milk, slamming the refrigerator door in the process. Newell looked up and said, "You're awfully grumpy this morning, Ernest. What's the matter? You swallow a hairball?"

Ernest shot him an icy glare. Then, suddenly, bubbling up from the depths of his stomach, came a loud guffaw. Then he started laughing. *Really* laughing.

Well, this caught Newell off guard and he started laughing too.

Somewhere, in the midst of all this, came a 'snort' from one, and then the other. This just triggered more laughter, and the two old men were brought to tears, holding their stomachs in pain. It was an effort to catch their breath, and finally the laughter quieted, then stopped. They just looked at each other, breathlessly smiling at the absurdity of this rare moment.

Then Newell got the hiccups.

This got them going again, and with every 'HYUCK!' the laughter got louder and louder, and the harder Newell tried to stop the spasms, the louder the 'HYUCKS' got.

Eventually, mercifully, the laughter subsided, and they wiped the tears from their eyes.

Max came in to see what all the commotion was about, and the morning returned to normal, with Ernest putting a bowl of cereal in front of Newell and pouring each of them a cup of coffee from the pot on the counter. There was no conversation, but every now and then they would look up at each other and smile at the memory of their rare, shared, moment of pure elation.

A laughing jag is better than a pill for what ails you.

Nap Time

Ernest had taken to watching soap operas every afternoon, although he'd never own up to it if anyone asked how he spent his days. He would sit in his worn and comfortable chair in the living room, his feet resting on the hassock, with a small lap robe draped over his knees.

Newell tried watching for a while, but all those risqué scenes made him squirmy, and it embarrassed him to be sitting across the room from his brother with all that heavy breathing going on. The stories didn't hold Ernest's attention for very long because every day, right around 2:30, his head would drop to his chest and he'd start snoring. He would stay sound asleep for at least an hour, sometimes an hour and a half. Once in a while, he would twitch with such a jerk that Newell swore he'd wake up, but he would go right on sleeping, dead to the world. Max napped right along with him, curled up on his lap.

Newell did crossword puzzles to pass the time. Ernest bought the books with the large format so his brother could see them better, and Newell had gotten pretty good at solving them, cheating only now and then when he got a clue like Trans Pyrenean Mmes.

He was in the kitchen working on a puzzle, Ernest's droning in the background lulling him into a slight stupor, when he got to the clue at 44 across: Artists of letters.

He knew the answer was calligraphers, but in the small squares, he printed, in capital letters, FRIED CHICKEN.

Newell hadn't driven a car for about six years, giving it up after one-too-many close calls and a visit from Billy Connors, a kid he had watched grow up from diapers, but who was now a sergeant on the local force. Billy had tried to be diplomatic at the time, explaining that, for his own safety and Ernest's peace of mind, he really shouldn't try getting behind the wheel anymore.

Billy wasn't quite prepared for such a volatile reaction from Newell, and he sat through a ten-minute tirade about the insolence of youth and lack of respect for the elderly. Newell had stood over Billy, sitting at the kitchen table, his face so close he could have bitten his nose off, and he might have if Billy wasn't wearing that badge. Finally, Billy told Newell, in no uncertain terms, that if he caught him driving anywhere, any time, he would throw him right in jail, and that was that.

There was a Kentucky Fried Chicken across town, not too far from the A&P. Newell had always groused about drive-up windows and how they just encouraged laziness. Banks, coffee shops, they all had them.

"What's next," he complained to Ernest, "drive up barbers?!"

They had a big old black Buick with wide whitewalls, still running pretty well, with just a bit of rust. Newell had inherited it from his uncle. It sat in the driveway, its nose facing the street. Ernest always backed it in so it would be easier to get the groceries out of the trunk.

Newell weighed the situation:

Ernest would be asleep for another hour or so. It was a straight shot over to White Avenue and then on to Park Street, up two sets of lights to Main, and there you were.

He walked over to the hook near the door and snapped up the car keys as if they were gold. He put on his light jacket and slowly, and

21

very carefully, using his walker, made his way to the car.

All the neighbors worked during the day, so he wasn't afraid of being spotted. He sat in the driver's seat and put his hands on the wheel, rubbing his bony fingers over the grooves he knew so well. He was about to turn the key in the ignition, but was afraid it might wake Ernest, so he put the big car into neutral and slowly coasted down to the end of the driveway and into the street. He started her up and headed toward White Avenue.

He had no apprehension at all about driving, although he knew his reflexes weren't what they used to be. He just had to make sure he didn't run into Billy Connors, or anything *else* for that matter.

It was a warm, sunny day in May, and he cranked the window down, almost running off the road with the effort. *"Take it slow, Newell,"* he said aloud. *"We can do this."*

He cruised along, enjoying the ride, the freedom, and the weather, when he spotted Gert Stimpson walking with Polly Grant past Martin's Bakery. He put his arm out the window and waved, yelling, "Hey, girls! How are ya?!"

They were too stunned to wave back and just watched as Newell barely made the turn at Park Street. Too late, he realized that if Ernest ran into Gert at the market she would spill the beans and…Well, he'd deal with that when the time came.

Now he was really grateful that Kentucky Fried Chicken had a drive-up. He certainly couldn't negotiate a bucket of chicken and his walker at the same time. He took a few leaves off the rhododendron border in the drive-up lane and pulled up to order. He watched the car in front of him so he would know what to do.

"May I take your order, please?" the machine shouted.

He was squinting at the menu board at the selections, cursing under his breath at all the choices. "Fried chicken," he yelled at the board.

"How many pieces, Sir?" the machine yelled back.

"How many can you get?" he yelled, noticing a line forming behind him.

"It's on the menu, sir." She was pleasant enough.

"I forgot my glasses. Help me out, will you?" he shouted, hoping no one recognized him.

"Two, three, or five, with a biscuit, or ten, fifteen, or twenty in a bucket, sir."

"Five is good," he said, hoping she heard him. He couldn't yell anymore.

"Anything to drink with that?"

"Nope, that's it," he said, wanting just to get the heck out of there. The line behind him had grown measurably, and he was starting to curse the damn drive-up system again.

"That'll be $5.59, sir. Please drive around."

His foot had fallen asleep, holding it on the break for just under five minutes, so when he went to move forward, the car lurched ahead with a jerk. Luckily, he had been there so long, there was no one in front of him. He slowly proceeded up to the window, paid the girl, and drove out onto Main Street, back toward the park.

Hatchard Park held a lot of fond memories for Newell. He and Catherine had spent many hours sitting on their special bench, feeding pigeons bread and crackers. This was where he kissed her for the first time, blushing and awkward, a nervous, gawky eighteen-year-old. They married a few years later, when she graduated from the university.

He pulled into the park and brought the car to a stop near the large tree that he had carved their initials in so many years ago. He could still make them out, high up, but just barely.

The aroma coming from the chicken was overwhelming, and he pushed the seat back, put the container between his legs, and took the first piece out, salivating madly. He burnt the roof of his mouth on the first bite, blew on it, then took his time, savoring each delicious morsel. It was wonderful, better than he had anticipated, and he was glad he had made the decision, reckless as it was, to satisfy his craving.

"Life's too short!" he said out loud as he pulled the Buick back out into traffic. He knew he had better get back to the house before Ernest woke up or there'd be hell to pay, but he decided to ride by the junior high on the way home to tap into another good memory.

Newell had been on the football team, The Chargers, and was pretty good, too. A photograph of him on one knee and holding his helmet had been displayed in a glass case on the first floor near the auditorium for the longest time, but he figured that, by now, what with all the renovation, it had been stored away someplace. Because of his short stint in high school, his glory days in uniform and cleats were something to hold onto.

He turned down Baker Street and drove slowly by the school, his mind flooded with memories, things he hadn't thought about in years. He would have parked next to the sidewalk and just sat there, thinking of old times and old victories, but he was already pushing it, so he left for home – nostalgic, but happy.

Suddenly, he realized he was lost. He found that he didn't know what street he was on, took a right onto a main road, and still had no idea where he was. He started talking to himself so he wouldn't panic and just kept driving, secretly wishing that Sergeant Connors would come cruising by, give him a lecture, and head him in the right direction.

Finally, he passed the library, and knew exactly where he was. He was closer to home than he had thought, and he drove slowly and carefully, very much looking forward to being there.

The tricky part would be backing into the driveway. He made the turn onto his street just as he saw the cruiser up the road, heading his way.

Ernest's baseball cap and sunglasses were on the seat, and Newell quickly put them on, slouched down in the seat, and waved at the officer as they passed each other. Luckily, it wasn't Billy, it was Earl Harnett, who would just think it was Ernest behind the wheel.

He angled the car out into the street, put it in reverse, and backed up slowly, right over the pansy bed on the left side of the driveway. He could tell the car wasn't straight, so he nosed it back into the street to try again. He had to rely on the rearview mirror, not being able to turn his head too far around, and gunned the Buick straight back, almost hitting the house.

He got out of the car, threw the hat and sunglasses back on the seat, and folded up the chicken container, bones and all, into half. He stuck it into the waist of his trousers and made his way up to the house. He hung up his jacket, put the keys back on the hook, and peeked around the corner to look for Ernest. He was snoring away, with Max still curled up on his lap.

Newell put the chicken bones, napkins, and container deep down in the trash can as quietly as he could, covering it all with paper towels and newspapers. He sat down to his crossword puzzle just as Max jumped down, waking Ernest from his sound sleep. She had smelled the chicken and came out to investigate.

"What have you been up to, Newell?" Ernest said, coming through the door, yawning. "Don't you get bored doing all those darn puzzles all the time?"

Newell looked up with a straight face and said, "Nope, not bored at all, Ernest. Not bored at all."

War, Torn

As a boy, Ernest was never resentful of Newell's athletic achievements. He was a tad jealous of all the attention he got, but he was also proud to be the brother of such a popular "jock" as those who excelled in football or basketball or track were called. He was a good head shorter than Newell and heavier in stature, but he never aspired to join the ranks of those who chose sports as their extracurricular activities. Nor was he a bookworm. Rather, he coasted through his school years, content with passing grades, never applying himself enough to achieve top grades or the honor roll.

Bess was a freckled red-headed girl who had had rather obvious romantic feelings toward Ernest since they were about eleven years old. Her heart would flutter whenever they passed in the school halls. He finally took notice when they were juniors, and his hormones finally caught up to hers.

They became inseparable. It was love. They were sure of it.

Her father had died when she was a small child and her mother raised her alone. She did a fine job, but Bess always had a vague feeling of insecurity without a father around. Perhaps it was a feeling she learned from her mother, although it was never spoken aloud. Ernest was her safe haven. She felt secure and protected by him.

She saved all of Ernest's tender love notes in a pretty wooden box, laminated with inlaid pieces of colored glass. She kept it locked under her bed.

Ernest saved up his allowance money and bought her a friendship ring, a sliver of silver with tiny hearts all around it. They pretended it was an engagement ring and made secret plans for a life together. Young love, so sweet, so perfect.

When they were seniors, all their classmates were buzzing about where they were going to college. One was almost expected to go on to higher education, and those who did not were subjected to a subtle distain.

There was a conflict overseas which, at first, was small and confined, but soon turned into a serious threat to America's allies. The United States became involved, though the outcome was far from certain. Knowing he did not have the grades to be admitted to college, and because his two best friends, Charlie and Angelo, had enlisted in the Army, Ernest made the decision to join them in their honorable pursuit.

Bess was devastated. He promised to return and they would be wed, but she was inconsolable. Surely, she argued, a trade school would give him a secure profession and keep him home and away from harm, but he was firm in his conviction, and, despite her tearful pleas, he left for boot camp shortly after graduation.

She wrote him letters every week, never knowing if they reached him, but every now and then, she would receive an airmail letter filled with loving words, along with a photograph of him looking handsome in his fatigues. His letters shielded her from the battlefield horrors he had seen, and he kept from her the sights and sounds that would haunt him for the rest of his life. She sent him a photograph of herself dressed in a summer frock with a ring of daisies in her hair. This sweet image of her kept his resolve strong to return and make her his wife. They would have babies. They would grow old together.

For two years they were apart, but his love for his precious Bess never wavered. In that foreign land, many temptations arose, but he remained ever faithful to his first and only love.

Eventually, her letters became less frequent. He tried to convince himself that, because his unit was always on the move, her letters were sitting in a pile in some Army Post Office. He tried to quell the sinking feeling that she had found a new love, that she had grown tired of the worry and the vast separation. His nights were tortured, picturing her in another man's arms. Every time a mail-call came, he expected the dreaded "Dear John" letter which would leave him a broken man.

Finally, her letters stopped. Another year passed, and his tour of duty was coming to an end. In his blinding sorrow, in order to save her the pain of having to pen "The Letter," he took the first step and wrote:

My Dear and Precious Bess,

I wish to inform you that I will be returning home soon, and in no way do I want you to feel obligated to return the affection we have shared in the past. I understand that much will have changed during our years apart, and I wish you every happiness. I will forever cherish our time together and hope you will always think fondly of me.

Yours truly, Ernest.

What he did not know, is that his letter was delivered to an empty house. During his lengthy absence, Bess had become terribly despondent and had become a recluse. By her own volition, emotionally crippled by nightmares and sadness, she was housebound. She, too, had suffered endless nights with no sleep, no respite from worry and fear, the stories of war chafing her ears and eyes daily. The evening news was filled with images of soldiers returning home with missing limbs or, worse, in flag-draped coffins. She had come to depend on her mother for comfort and solace.

One cold and cloudy winter morning, Bess came downstairs to find her mother on the kitchen floor, lifeless. She had suffered a cerebral hemorrhage, a stroke. Her body was rigid and cold, and her eyes were open. No amount of shaking her could bring her back.

Bess called the emergency number, frantically screaming into the phone for help, but that was the last thing she was ever able to do. Upon losing her mother, her only source of support and sanity, and overcome with grief, she suffered a severe mental breakdown. The loss of her dear mother, combined with the long separation from her loving Ernest, was too great, her sorrow too heavy to bear. She was placed in an institution and was gently cared for, but she never regained a sense of herself. This bright, red-haired girl-turned-woman was a mere shell of what was.

Ernest returned home to this news and rushed to her side at the home. As he took her hands in his and looked into her beautiful green eyes, he was met with a blank stare, with not even a blink of recognition. Astonished by the severity of her condition, he asked to speak to the matron of the ward and was told there was little to no hope for a recovery. Then the woman opened a drawer next to where Bess was sitting, reached in, and took out the box containing all of his love letters, penned with youthful passion.

With tears in his eyes, he gently kissed Bess's face, her hair, her hands, and left, his heart forever shattered.

Ernest never married. After his discharge from the service, he completed three years of apprenticeship, then secured a position as a carpenter's assistant. He eventually opened his own shop, hiring two men, and ran a very successful business which quickly gained, and retained, the respect of the community.

Now, every so often, in the privacy of his room, he opens his wallet and takes out the faded and worn photograph of his one and only love, his dear Bess. He brings it to his lips, and remembers, sadly, the joy she brought him, so long ago.

Battlegrounds long past, his love, long gone, Ernest has occasional nightmares of mortar fire, but, mercifully, more often, he dreams of the pretty girl in the summer dress. Of young love and all that it promised.

Isabella

The brothers lived in the house where Newell and Catherine had spent their married years. They had bought the big house expecting to have children, but she had lost a baby through miscarriage when she was twenty-six, and another several years later, quite far along in the pregnancy. Although she was deeply in love with Newell, these losses were devastating to her, and after the second, she gently declined further intimacy. She couldn't bear the loss of yet another child, and, regretfully, put an end to that possibility. As difficult as this was for Newell to understand, he loved her dearly and so he accepted and honored her decision.

It was a two-story white house with black shutters in a nondescript style, set up on a slight rise. It had two bedrooms and a half-bath on the second floor, and a living room, kitchen, den, and full bath downstairs. The brothers' bedrooms rooms were side by side at the opposite end of the house from the kitchen.

Catherine had taken pride in her home and had decorated it in a traditional style, with wallpaper throughout and pretty lace curtains at the windows. There were oriental and braided rugs in most of the rooms, and collectable knick-knacks were lovingly placed here and there. A spinet piano sat in the corner of the living room. Catherine played classical music until her illness prevented it, and Newell especially loved hearing her play Mozart's lively *Rondo alla Turca* and Beethoven's gentle *Für Elise*.

Ernest reluctantly moved in after she died out of a sense of obligation, but also out of a never-spoken affection for his older brother. He cared for him, always had, but Newell made it clear that he would begrudgingly share his home. With all his aches and pains, his lack of mobility, and the loss of his wife, Newell had become a bitter man. He had never told his brother how Catherine had curtailed the tender, yet passionate physical bond they had shared because her grief over losing her babies was stronger than her desire for him. Of how it had been nearly impossible not to reach for her as they slept together in the same bed, night after night, for all those years. And – Newell's own heart-wrenching sorrow stemming from the loss of his unborn children went largely unacknowledged because of Catherine's dire need to be comforted. Somehow, in circumstances such as this, the father's grief takes a back seat to the mother's. He couldn't express his heartache, and he showed a brave face to the world, but a part of him died with his children. All this private pain was the genesis of his negative attitude toward life.

Out of necessity, most of the housework fell on Ernest, while Newell's chores consisted of cleaning the kitchen counter and sink, the downstairs bathroom vanity and sink, and doing the dishes, all of which he could do while leaning against the counters. He didn't mind it. He just took his time and it got done.

In later years, Ernest found the work of dusting, washing, and vacuuming the floors and doing the laundry more and more difficult, and he had begun neglecting some of the chores out of sheer fatigue and a nagging pain in his lower back. Once, Newell, seeing a film of dust on an end table in the living room, printed a big HELLO in it with his finger. It took a couple of days before Ernest noticed it, and once he did, he let Newell hear about it.

One morning, Newell was at the sink doing the breakfast dishes when he spotted an unfamiliar car across the street in the driveway. He watched as a short stout woman with dark hair pulled up in a bun got out, went to the trunk, and unloaded a vacuum cleaner and a large plastic basket filled with cleaning supplies. She made her way up the driveway and entered the house with a key.

"Ernest, the Andersons have a housekeeper!" Newell yelled to the living room where Ernest was watching the news on TV. He came into the kitchen and stood next to Newell at the window and looked at the light blue sedan with great interest.

That night, as they were eating their Salisbury Steak dinners, Ernest said, "Newell, what do you think about us hiring a housekeeper? I'm not as young as I used to be, and I'm finding I can't keep up like before."

Newell, picking up a forkful of mealy beef, said, "It would cost extra money that we don't have, Ernest."

Ernest replied, "Well, I haven't told you, but I have been putting money away every so often for a rainy-day fund. It's been just sitting in a Christmas Club in Harper Federal, and I think this would be a fine way to use it. But, only if you agree."

They never agreed on *anything*, so this was a new wrinkle. After a long pause, Newell said, "All right, let's give it a shot."

Two weeks later, the car appeared in the driveway again. Ernest had been keeping an eye out, and he threw on his jacket and quickly walked across the street as the woman was unloading her car.

"Hello! My name is Ernest Madison. I live across the street in that white house with my brother, and we were wondering if you had any openings for cleaning? I find that it's becoming too much for me," he said with a touch of embarrassment.

She turned to him with a smile and said, "I am Isabella," and warmly shook his hand.

"Your timing, it is good, Mr. Madison. I just have lost a client. She is with the angels, so, yes, I do have a space for you. When I am finished my work here, I will come across and look at your house and give to you an estimate," she said with a slight accent.

"That will be fine. Thank you," he said, and walked back across the street.

About an hour and a half later, there was a gentle knock on the door and Ernest showed Isabella into the kitchen. The three of them sat at the table, and Isabella explained that she was Portuguese and had come to America from Valadares, Portugal, a small parish just inland from the Atlantic, when she was nineteen years of age, to marry a boy who had been chosen for her by her parents.

She looked to be in her mid-fifties. Her flawless skin showed no signs of age, with nary a line, but her hands bore evidence of a life of labor. She wore no makeup, and she had deep, dark brown eyes with long black lashes. She was not a particularly pretty woman, but she had a subtle grace about her.

Max had felt the presence of someone in the house and came out to investigate. She jumped up on the kitchen table and went right over to this new person and nuzzled Isabella's cheek.

"Its name?" she asked, patting Max's head.

"Max," Newell answered.

"Olá, Max. Very nice it is to make your acquaintance," she said, and Max purred and nuzzled her face again.

They agreed on a price, a price that surprised the brothers who had thought it would be far more expensive for what she would do. She would come every other week, on Tuesdays, at 9:00 in the morning. Ernest gave her the spare key that was hanging on the hook near the door.

As she was leaving, he said, "Gracias, Isabella."

34

She turned to him with a smile, and said, "The Portuguese word for thank you is 'obrigado.' And, you are most welcome."

He blushed and showed her to the door.

Isabella was a FORCE.

She made her way around the house with incredible stamina: dusting, wiping down every surface in sight, dust-mopping and washing the floors, picking up newspapers that had piled up on the floor or the hassock, cleaning both toilets and the bathtub, and putting dirty clothes in the hamper, singing softly in Portuguese all the while.

The brothers did not know what to do with themselves and tried to keep out of her way, moving from room to room as she methodically worked her way around the house. Max made herself scarce, too.

It seemed strangely wonderful to have this woman around. She had a positive energy about her, and it was infectious. Isabella brought a welcome change to their mundane routine.

One morning they had gone food shopping and came back as Isabella was cleaning in the kitchen. Newell went into the living room to sit down and rest, and Ernest began to unload the groceries. As he placed a couple of TV dinners on the counter, she said to him, in an incredulous tone, "You eat *those*?"

"Yes, I'm a lousy cook, and Newell isn't *able* to cook, and these are easy," he replied, shrugging his shoulders.

She gave him a slight frown and said, "I bring you something next time I come. Anything you are not supposed to eat?"

"No, uh, uh, no," he stammered, trying to think of a way to tell her she really didn't have to bother, but the moment passed, and she went about her business.

Later that night he told Newell what she had said. They both felt pangs of fear, worrying about what exotic flavors and strange spices she would put in the food that she would bring to them. They were raised to be gentlemen, but they wondered how they could let her know that they hated the food without hurting her feelings, and the thought of eating this foreign fare out of sheer politeness was *very* disconcerting. They were of Northern European descent, and the food they had eaten all their lives was what was referred to as, 'Meat and Potatoes,' meaning no spices, no sauces. In a word – bland.

They were nervous.

When Isabella came two weeks later, after unpacking her cleaning supplies, she went back out to her car and brought in a large disposable aluminum pan covered with foil, and a loaf of braided bread, its golden crust peeking out of a wrapping of white paper, and placed them on the counter. Strange and intense aromas hit the two immediately, and they began salivating at the smell of garlic and onions, and some kind of mysterious spices.

"Caldo Verde," she said, as she peeled back the aluminum foil a bit so they could take a peek.

"Place this in the refrigerator and remove it one half of an hour before you wish to eat. Heat it, without its cover, at three hundred and fifty degrees in your oven for thirty-five minutes, or until it makes bubbles at its edges."

"What is it?" Newell said, trying not to sound rude, but failing.

"Portuguese sausage and vegetables," she said with a smile. "It is good. Have it with my bread. It is good." As she was leaving for the day, she said to them, "Ha, ha! No television dinners tonight!" and shut the door behind her, laughing.

"This is the most delicious thing I have ever tasted in my LIFE!"

Ernest exclaimed as he dipped a second piece of bread into the thick tomato broth brimming with potatoes, chorizo, onions, garlic, and kale.

"I thought we'd hate it!" Newell said with a giddy smile on his face.

They nearly devoured the whole, beautiful loaf of sweet bread, and a good portion of the hearty stew before they finally pushed themselves away from the table, groaning.

Thereafter, every two weeks, which seemed like an eternity to them, Newell and Ernest would enjoy delightful new flavors and swoon at the aromas wafting from dishes like Bacalhau, a dish of codfish, potatoes, eggs, onions, and garlic; Piri Piri Chicken, an amazing amalgam of pieces of chicken, lemon, wine, paprika, and piri piri, a spicy pepper; and sometimes just sandwiches, made with hard cheese and Jamón Ibérico, a luxurious cured ham which, Isabella explained, came from free-roaming pigs which grazed in oak-studded fields and ate grass and acorns. These would be accompanied by crispy fried potatoes.

It was bi-monthly, gustatory heaven. Her passion for cooking was obvious, and she took great pleasure in knowing that her clients, whom she affectionately called, 'meus rapazes,' (my boys), were relishing her endeavors.

It never ceased to surprise the brothers that they would be enjoying a cuisine that would be considered quite spicy by local norms, and they were quite happy about it, and also, that neither of them had a delicate stomach.

However, their blissful food adventure nearly came to an abrupt end when Isabella brought Feijoada de Lulas, a dish of squid, its tentacles menacingly tucked in amongst pinto beans and cilantro. Ernest actually jumped back as he pulled the foil off the pan, reminded of a movie he had seen: *20,000 Leagues Under the Sea* starring Kirk Douglas, wherein a monstrous giant squid threatens a marine biologist and his hapless crew.

Politeness be damned, neither brother could bring himself to tuck into the apparition before them. Ernest put the pan aside and heated up a couple of cans of beef stew that night, and when Isabella asked how they liked her dish the next time she came, Ernest said, simply, that it didn't agree with them, patting his belly with the inside of his fist, and puffing his cheeks to mimic a burp. Her pride was spared, and they were relieved to know that they would not have to face that dreaded sea creature again.

They rarely had dessert after dinner, but they couldn't resist Isabella's delightful Tibias de Braga, a type of cream-filled pastry similar to a cream puff, or her custard tart, Pastel de Nata. Previously, their idea of a tasty dessert was instant tapioca pudding topped with Cool Whip.

One morning, Isabella explained the origin of many of Portugal's rich confections and breads. Traditionally, she said, egg whites were used as a starch for nuns' robes and priests' clothing, so there was always an abundance of left-over egg yolks in the village kitchens, the result of which were these beautiful pastries and loaves, the recipes passed down from generation to generation over the centuries.

Over the course of several months, not surprisingly, Ernest and Newell gained several pounds. The extra weight looked good on Newell because he was tall and always quite thin, but Ernest just got rounder. Neither one complained. It was all good.

Life at home was better, but there was still tension between the brothers, and their arguments often led to long silences. But, at dinner, with Isabella's tantalizing food in front of them, it was always pleasant and calm. A welcome change, indeed.

A Full Circle

Catherine had been a good cook. Nothing fancy, just good plain cooking. Most wives, who made up the majority of homemakers, cooked the same meals week after week:

Monday: Chicken; Tuesday: Pork chops; Wednesday: Spaghetti with sauce; Thursday: Meatloaf; and Friday: Fish. Saturdays might be hotdogs or hamburgers, and Sundays always featured a roast with vegetables.

Not Catherine. She liked to change it up. She had several cookbooks – Betty Crocker and Fannie Farmer having the most stained and worn pages – and she had saved many hand-written recipe cards of much-loved dishes her mother had fed to her own family. Newell never knew what he might have for dinner on any given night. He loved being surprised, and she loved surprising him.

She would always bring the same casserole to potluck suppers. It consisted of chicken, potatoes, and mixed vegetables in a creamy sauce. Whenever she was asked for the recipe, which was quite often, she would smile and say, "I can't give away my secret ingredient!"

Once, when she was failing and near the end of her life, Newell asked her if she would tell him the secret ingredient. Weakly, and with a sly grin, she leaned toward him and whispered, "Campbell's Cream of Celery Soup!"

He forced a smile and said, "Thank you, Dear. My lips are sealed."

After she passed, Newell's eating habits went sharply downhill. He couldn't, and wouldn't, cook for himself. For a time, kind neighbors and friends would bring covered dishes over, but it was a real effort for him to divide them up into individual servings and freeze them, which is what he did for a short while. He had no energy and no motivation.

After a couple of weeks, the meals stopped coming, which is what happens after a death. There is a great rush, in the beginning, to want to help the grieving spouse, but it dwindles over time, and then stops. People go about their lives, assuming the need has passed and all is well, when it is anything but. And Newell was too proud to reach out for help.

He started relying on canned foods and the ubiquitous TV dinners. He would often skip breakfast and simply forget to have lunch. He was alone, lonely, and he hated it. Food was the last thing on his mind.

He began to lose weight. He had always been rather thin and lanky, but now his pants were hanging a bit lower and his face was gaunt. He also had fallen a few times. Ernest noticed a bruise on his arm one day during lunch at Millie's and asked him about it. He finally confessed that he had taken a tumble.

That is when Ernest knew he had to move in. He knew it wouldn't be easy on either of them, their relationship was tenuous at best, but there was really no choice – Newell could no longer live alone. Ernest moved out of his small apartment across town and settled in to the big old house with Newell, knowing it would be a bumpy ride.

And that it was. Before Isabella entered their lives, Newell took his frustration about aging and his infirmity out on Ernest, and Ernest resented having to take care of his ungrateful brother. Isabella had brought a modicum of peace to their home.

While getting dressed in his bedroom one morning, Newell felt his wedding ring slip off his finger onto the floor. He slowly reached down, put it in the palm of his hand, gently touched it, and his heart was flooded with wonderful memories of the many decades spent with his beloved Catherine. Inside the band, well-worn but still visible, was an engraving of a tiny sun and moon. "You are my sun and my moon," was the special phrase they would say to each other when they were courting, and for all the years thereafter. He didn't dare put it back on his finger, afraid that he would lose it somewhere, so he reluctantly placed the ring on the back of the tall bureau, behind her framed photograph.

Isabella was a godsend. Over time, she had told the brothers stories of her life, and they had shared bits and pieces of theirs. She told them that she had fought her arranged marriage to no avail. In the beginning, it had been extremely awkward to be with someone she barely knew, but she had come to love her husband, Paulo, deeply. He was a good man, a good father, and loved their sons as fiercely as she did. He had a painting and wallpapering business and had developed a loyal and steady clientele in town. They were in a good place, and she was happy and content.

She loved bringing meals over for the two brothers. It was no bother, really. She simply made extra of whatever she made for her family on any given Monday night and packed it up for cleaning day.

As she was vacuuming in Newell's bedroom one day, Isabella heard a clanking from the machine. She quickly shut it off, took a paper shopping bag from a cabinet in the kitchen, and went out to the side lawn with the vacuum. She knelt down and reached into the vacuum bag, placing the dusty contents into the paper bag, one careful handful at a time. Finally, she saw it: a gold ring, shining in the sun. Apparently, she was dusting the bureau one day and had knocked the ring to the floor without knowing it. It had been there for quite a while, in the small space between the wall and the rug.

Newell was sitting in the living room reading the paper when she entered, clutching the ring in her hand. "Mr. Newell, this was in your bedroom. My vacuum found it. You have, perhaps, been missing it?"

Not knowing what she held, he opened his hand, and she placed the ring in his palm. She saw his eyes redden and quickly left the room. He looked down at the ring and tears filled his eyes. He sat there, weeping softly for a few minutes, then slid the ring onto his finger.

"It fits!" he cried. The weight he had gained from Isabella's robust meals had plumped his finger enough so that the ring fit perfectly.

"Gosh almighty, I will never take this off again!" he said, smiling broadly and laughing, wiping his eyes with his sleeve.

Isabella overheard him from the kitchen and was smiling too, as she put her vacuum back together and continued her cleaning, softly singing in her native language.

And she thought: "*Hoje é um bom dia*" – Today is a good day.

One Minute

Isabella let herself in on cleaning day and heard Ernest and Newell carping at each other in the living room. She shook her head as she unpacked her cleaning supplies and began her work. Their bickering was a common occurrence in this house, and she found herself thinking about it more and more. Even at home, she found herself feeling sad for the brothers. She decided to try, in some small way, to mend fences. She was a shy woman, but her feelings ran deep, and she felt compelled to interfere, regardless of the possible repercussions. Taking a deep breath, she walked into the living room and excused herself, saying, "Please to forgive my intrusion into your private matters, but I feel that I must speak."

They stopped arguing and gave her their full attention, standing up as she said, "You both have more days behind you than you have ahead of you. You have lived longer than you will live. You waste much precious time with your quarreling. The frustrations of advancing age have hardened your hearts and there is great bitterness here. If one of you were to go to the angels, the other will be left alone. *All alone.*"

She paused to determine if she had overstepped a boundary, but seeing no negative reaction on their faces, she continued:

"My precious sons, Eduardo and Luis, were like you when they were young boys. They have the same number of years between them – six. They fought all of the time! My heart breaks to think of them at the end of their lives, like the two of you, resenting each other and

43

having this coldness between them."

"Mr. Ernest, about what did you quarrel with your brother yesterday?"

Ernest thought for a moment, and said, "Ah, er, I don't remember."

Isabella then said, "Mr. Newell, what was it that you and your brother disagreed about two days ago?"

Newell was sure he could remember and paused as he tried to think of what it was.

When he said nothing, she said, "This is what I made my boys do when I had had enough of their nonsense. Since you behave like children, I will insist that you do it too. Please to come with me."

She then took the brothers by their elbows and led them into the kitchen. She pulled two chairs from under the table, placed them facing each other, and motioned for each brother to sit down, knees to knees. They obeyed, curious as to what would come of this strange request.

"Now – you will look into each other's eyes for one minute. One *full* minute without looking away." She watched the red clock on the wall until the second hand reached twelve, and said, "Now."

Tick – tick – tick…

Three seconds… Ten seconds…

At about fourteen seconds they broke eye contact, squirming in their chairs and looking away, Ernest laughing nervously.

Newell said, "This is crazy!"

And Ernest said, "I can't do this. What are you trying to do here, Isabella?"

She said nothing and gestured with a finger to be silent. They felt a bit like children being scolded by their mother for some long-forgotten infraction, but they allowed her to continue out of respect for this gentle woman who had, thus far, changed their lives in a such a positive way.

She started timing them again.

It was an *eternity*. It was uncomfortable and awkward and *painfully* intimate, but they held their gaze. Near the end of the sixty seconds, after what seemed to be an hour, a tear trickled down Newell's cheek, and Ernest's eyes had reddened.

It was as if centuries of built-up grime and a thick, ancient crust had been chipped away at an archaeological dig. A metaphorical amulet, glistening in the sun, showed itself.

Newell slowly leaned forward and put one hand on Ernest's knee. Ernest reached down and put his hand over Newell's gnarly fingers. They had no words. They were both overcome with emotion.

Isabella quietly went to the counter and cut two pieces of her delectable pastry, 'the cream puff cake' as they called it. She placed the plates on the table in front of them and said, gently, "You, in this moment, have looked into each other's *souls*, and you have seen the beauty and the love that resides within. Do not forget this day."

She left the room to begin her cleaning, and they ate in silence, glancing up at each other now and then with a subtle trace of a smile, their emotions still fragile.

Their spats didn't end completely, not by any means, but they definitely had softened toward each other, and there was more laughter in the house than there had ever been in all their time together. And Isabella felt joy in her heart, knowing that her delicate plan had been successful.

Love, a precious artifact long buried, saw the light of day again.

The Doctor is 'In'

Ernest was passing by Newell's bedroom one January morning on the way to the kitchen and saw him sitting at the edge of his bed with his elbows on his knees and his head down.

"Newell, are you okay?"

"I'm fine."

"You sure?" Ernest asked with concern in his voice.

Newell said, "I just got a little lightheaded is all. I'm *fine!*"

He'd been getting a bit woozy for the past couple of months but didn't want to tell Ernest because he knew he wouldn't let it go. He wasn't worried about it. To him, it was just another one of life's aggravations.

A few days later, they were getting ready to go to Millie's just before noon, and as Newell was putting on his coat, he staggered and nearly fell against the kitchen counter. Ernest caught his arm, steadied him, and led him to a chair.

"Okay, what's going on with you, Newell?"

"I just felt a little faint, nothing to worry about, Ernest," he said, angry that he had been caught in another dizzy spell.

"That's it. You're going to the doctor. When's the last time you went, anyway?" Ernest asked.

"I don't know!" Newell said, angrily. "Before she passed, Catherine made me promise to get a check-up. I had my fingers crossed when I agreed. I never got around to it."

46

"My goodness, Mr. Madison, you haven't been here in four years!" the pretty young receptionist said as they stood at the counter. "You'll need to fill out these forms, please," and she handed him a clipboard with several sheets of paper on it.

He had left his glasses home again and passed the board to Ernest. "Here. Can you fill this out for me? You know all there is to know, well, mostly."

They sat in the waiting room, and Ernest began to fill out the forms. Newell grabbed a magazine from a table next to his chair but threw it back down when he realized he couldn't read it anyway.

He looked around the room where several people were seated, awaiting their turn to see the doctor. "There's all *old* people here," he whispered, quite loudly, to Ernest, who was busy writing.

Ernest gestured to him to shush.

"Ernest, that picture on the wall…"

"No! Leave it," said Ernest.

Finally a nurse opened a door across the room and said, "Newell Madison?"

As he stood up with the help of his cane and made his way over to the doorway, Ernest said, "Newell, do you want me to come in with you?"

He would have cursed if there weren't people in the waiting room, but Newell said, "No, I'm good."

"Follow me," the nurse said. "My name is Jenny. Let's get you weighed."

She gently took his arm and helped him step up onto the scale. As she started to run the metal slide down the bar, he said, "You're gonna weigh me with my coat on? And my boots?"

She smiled and said, "That's right."

He said, "So, if I come back next summer, and you weigh me with no coat and no boots, you're gonna say, "Why, Mr. Madison, you've lost weight!"

She smiled again, and said, "It's okay. We allow for that."

"Makes no damn sense," he mumbled under his breath.

She led him down the hall to an exam room, closed the door behind them, helped him take his coat off, and said, "I need to get your vitals. Please roll up your sleeve," as she reached for the blood pressure cuff. She helped him up onto the examination table, took his temperature and blood pressure, and placed a plastic clamp on his finger.

"What's *that* for?" he snapped, realizing that he sounded pretty cranky.

"This is to check your oxygen level. To see if you're still alive!" she said with a laugh, trying to break the tension. He didn't smile, and she said, "Here's a johnny for you. Everything off but your underwear, opening in the back."

"Why the heck do I have to put a johnny on? I have a hell of a time getting my pants on and off, and you'll have to take off my boots! Can't I just take my shirt off and put the johnny on over my trousers?"

She hesitated, then said, "That will be fine," as she bent down to remove his boots. "The doctor will be in to see you shortly," she said as she left the room.

He sat at the edge of the exam table, and said loudly, "It's freezing in here!" He couldn't reach around to tie the johnny, so his whole back was exposed, and he was shivering.

He looked around the small, windowless room at the various instruments hanging on the wall. Out of curiosity, he leaned over to touch one of the cords and nearly fell off the table. Scanning the room, he saw a calendar, a chart of the human body, and the counter was filled with jars of cotton balls, boxes of latex gloves, and various tubes of what, he didn't know. His eyes landed on several framed graduation certificates with a doctor's name printed in perfect calligraphy, reminding him of the crossword puzzle that led him on his driving escapade, and he raised his eyebrows and grinned, guiltily, at the memory. One of the certificates was crooked, but he didn't dare get off the table to straighten it for fear of falling.

"Newell Madison," the doctor said, briskly entering the room. "May I call you Newell?" he asked.

"Might as well," Newell answered. "That's my name."

"I'm Dr. Magnuson, but you can call me Dr. Magnuson," the doctor said, making a small attempt at humor to break the ice. When Newell didn't smile, he just cleared his throat and reached for the stethoscope which was hanging on a hook on the wall.

Newell's head was spinning because the doctor didn't look a day over nineteen to him. He was trying to do the math in his head: Four years of undergraduate study; four years of medical school; at least three years as a resident...

Not caring if he sounded rude, he said, "Doc, how old are you, anyway?"

The doctor said, "Thirty-two, the last time I checked. Why do you ask?"

Newell shook his head and said, "You look like a kid, is all. I guess I'm just an old geezer. Even the cops look like high school kids to me."

"So, what brings you in, Newell?"

"My brother made me come. Nothing wrong with me," he said, with a distinct edge to his voice.

The doctor asked him questions about his diet, exercise, and sleep habits as he proceeded with his exam, looking into Newell's ears with the otoscope, having him stick out his tongue and say, "Ahh," and

49

listening to his chest and back with the stethoscope saying, "Deep breath. Another one." Every time he touched the stethoscope to his back, Newell jumped.

"That thing is freezing!" he said. "And it's freezing in this room! Why do they keep it so damn cold?"

Dr. Magnuson said, "It keeps the germs down. We'll be done shortly. I need to check the circulation in your feet. Any cramping or numbness?"

"Nope," Newell replied, crossing his fingers behind his back.

"Do you have any aches and pains?" the doctor continued.

"My brother is a pain, if that counts," Newell said with a toothy grin, hoping to sound a little nicer than he had previously.

The doctor smiled and said, "Here, let me help you off the table and we'll do the rectal exam."

Newell forgot about this nasty bit of business – it had been so long.

The doctor said, "Undo your pants and bend over please."

This happened to be on a Wednesday, which meant that the night before, Tuesday night, was when he had feasted on one of Isabella's wonderful creations. And, it so happened, that last night's dinner was Arroz com Frango, a rich rice and *bean* dish. As the doctor was putting on a glove and about to insert his finger, Newell suddenly felt the urge to pass gas. He tightened his sphincter as hard as he could, praying desperately for control.

The doctor felt the muscle contract around his finger, and said, "Relax Newell, this only takes a second."

Mercifully it was over and done, with no flatulence to embarrass him, but he felt his stomach rumble.

The doctor said, "You can get dressed now. We'll send you downstairs for some lab work. I'll have Jenny call you when we get the results."

"My boots," Newell said, pointing to them.

Dr. Magnuson helped him put them back on, saying, "I must say, Newell, you seem to be in remarkably good health for a man of your age. Must be clean living!" and he shook his hand and left the room.

Newell chuckled and said to himself, "Clean living, indeed."

Little did the doctor know that every night after dinner, Newell had two fingers of bourbon with a couple of ice cubes, and that he had started smoking at age fourteen and didn't quit until he was in his mid-sixties, sick of tasting like an ashtray when he woke up in the morning. When he decided to quit, he tossed his cigarettes in the trash and never looked back. Also, his nightly bowl of ice cream probably wouldn't have passed muster either.

After the bloodwork, the brothers walked back out to the car, and, as Ernest held the door for him, Newell plopped down on the seat with a relieved sigh. No sooner had Ernest gotten in and closed the door, when Newell let go with a long, loud fart.

"Jayzus, Newell! What the hell?" Ernest said, quickly rolling the window down.

Newell just said, "Sorry. Better you than him," and relaxed into the seat.

About a week later, Jenny called. She said, "Good news, Mr. Madison. Your symptoms and blood work indicate that you have a Vitamin B deficiency, and you are slightly anemic. The doctor wants you to take a multivitamin every day, with iron, and B-12 for a few weeks."

"No prescriptions?" he asked.

"No, just some vitamins. That's all you need. Have a great day, now!"

Newell knew he had dodged a bullet. Most of his friends were long dead, and the ones who were still alive seemed to have one foot on a banana peel.

That night, sitting in his chair in the living room, he took a long, slow sip of his Jim Beam and sighed, glad that the day's ordeal was over. The cat jumped up on his lap, and he said, "I live to see another day, Max."

Then he remembered the car fart and started laughing.

Ernest heard him from the other room, and said, "What's so funny in there, brother?"

"Just something on TV, Ernest. Just something on TV."

Closet Clutter

It was a cold February day, and Newell was sitting in the living room working on a crossword puzzle. It felt a little chilly in the house, so he put the lap-robe over his legs.

Ernest had just come in from shoveling the front steps. It had snowed the night before, and he wanted to get to it before it froze solid. This winter had been unusually cold, and the wind outside cut like a knife.

"Sheesh, it's cold out there," he said, walking through the room and hanging his coat in the closet. "I need to buy one of those stocking things that goes over your head and covers everything but your eyes and mouth. What the heck do you call it?"

"It sounds like that Greek dessert, Baklava," Newell said, looking up from his puzzle.

As much as Ernest teased him about doing his crosswords, he had learned a lot from them. Whenever there was a word that he couldn't get, he would look it up in the dictionary, and it usually found a place in his memory bank. Baklava was one of them.

"Balaclava! That's it," Ernest said. "I'll have to see if Hoffman's carries them, but I doubt it. Maybe the sporting goods store."

Ernest sat down in his chair and took the book he was reading off the end table just as Max came into the room and jumped up on his lap.

"What the...?!" The cat's feet were soaking wet, and he quickly pushed her onto the floor.

"Newell, did Max get outside? She's all wet!"

"No, she's been here all morning. Why don't you follow her tracks and see if you can figure out where she got wet? I know she wouldn't have peed on the floor!" (He was always defending her).

Ernest stood up to look, but the way the light was coming in the window made it difficult to see any tracks. He went into the kitchen and grabbed the flashlight out of the junk drawer and came back in to search.

"Here we go," he said, as he followed wet paw tracks into the den. There, he saw a small puddle on the floor in front of the closet. He opened the door, and saw water stains on some boxes that were stored on the floor.

"We have a burst pipe, dammit!" he yelled to Newell. "We'll have to call a plumber. What a pain!"

The Richard's Plumbing van pulled up in front later that afternoon. A burst pipe was considered an emergency, so he got there as soon as he could. His name was Richard Richards, which was kind of a local joke. You didn't know which Richard was on the truck, his first or his last name.

"I'm going to have to cut through the wall in the closet," Richard said to the brothers, holding his flashlight in his hand. Sorry, but you're going to have to move all that stuff out of the way. I'll shut the water off, and I'll be back tomorrow morning, first thing."

After he left, Ernest mopped up the water and began pulling boxes out of the closet. He opened the wet boxes first and saw that they held old 33 1/3" vinyl records, sheet music – from when Catherine played the piano, and menus and matchbook covers from restaurants, now long gone. He got a sheet from the armoire in his bedroom and put it over his bed to protect the bedspread, and went into the den for the dry boxes.

"Newell, come in here. We're going to have to go through these boxes and get rid of some stuff. Some of this has been in here for years!"

There were shoeboxes full of photographs and a pile of board games including Parcheesi, Monopoly, Chinese Checkers, Clue, Scrabble, and several decks of playing cards. There was a ten-pin bowling ball in its carrying case, a pair of men's bowling shoes, and a large white box wrapped in a white ribbon.

They began going through the photographs and realized that Catherine had kept them for decades. There were pictures of the brothers as children, on vacation at either a lake or a pond. They looked to be about six and twelve years old and were standing side-by-side on a dock, holding small sunfish they had caught. They had big smiles on their faces and were sunburned. There were photos of their parents, aunts, uncles, and cousins. They all used to go away together, and these prints brought back wonderful memories. They didn't have much money, but their parents managed to get them away on small trips every summer.

"We were happy kids, weren't we?" Newell said.

"That's for sure," Ernest replied. "The good old days really were the good old days."

They spent a good hour looking through the photographs, reminiscing about their enjoyable childhood experiences, then Newell turned to the big white box. He untied the satin ribbon and opened it. He pulled away layers of white tissue paper and uncovered Catherine's wedding dress. Laying on top of it was a framed photograph of the two of them on their wedding day. There was a gray velvet bow tie in the upper corner of the box. He took in a quick breath and struggled to maintain his composure.

Looking at the photograph, he remembered the feel of his navy-blue, double-breasted jacket and trousers. There was a white rose boutonnière on his lapel, and he was wearing the gray bow tie.

Catherine was radiant in her beautiful white gown. It had a tea-length tulle skirt, a long-sleeved lace bodice with a scoop neckline, and a silk flower at the waist. She wore a shoulder-length tulle veil and held a bouquet of white roses and baby's breath. Scent-memory is a powerful thing, and he could smell the heady aroma of the roses.

There they were: two, fresh-faced 23-year-olds, about to embark on a glorious journey – a marriage that would last forever. They were beaming.

Ernest saw the emotion on Newell's face and asked if he wanted him to take the dress out to look at it, but Newell shook his head, and said, "No. I've seen enough." He got up, left the room, and went back to his chair in the living room. He didn't pick up his crossword puzzle again that night. He just sat in silence, reminiscing.

The next day, bright and early, Richard came back. He cut out a hole in the closet wall, repaired the broken pipe, and patched the hole with a piece of plywood. In his shop, he had made a 30-inch-long platform out of two-by-fours, placed it on the closet floor, and said to Ernest, "You might want to put those boxes on this in case of another leak. Just kidding! I fix leaks, I don't cause 'em, but better safe than sorry," he said with a laugh. Ernest thanked him, paid him in cash, and Richard left.

"So, what do you think about everything in those boxes?" Ernest asked, heading into his room. "Anything you want to keep?"

Newell thought for a moment and said, "The records, the sheet music, the menus, and the bowling stuff can go. The photographs and dress don't take up much room. They can stay."

"And the games? Hey, how about a game of Monopoly tonight?"

Newell said, "That game takes *hours* to play!"

Ernest replied, "Well, I don't have a train to catch, do you?"

And so they played Monopoly that night, and Parcheesi another night, and then they broke out Scrabble, and their evenings were full for quite a long time.

And the sweet scent of white roses stayed with Newell for quite a long time, as well.

Of Goatees and Goats

Late one morning, Ernest noticed that Newell was looking a little shaggy. He said, "Are you planning on shaving today, Newell?"

"None of your business!" Newell said, harshly, and Ernest just sighed and walked away.

A few days went by, and it was apparent that Newell still hadn't shaved. Ernest knew if he breached the subject again, he would get a snarky reaction, but they would be going to Millie's in a day or two, and Ernest was concerned that people might think Newell was losing it. He had always been clean-shaven and dressed neatly, even when he was home for the day.

As he sat down for breakfast, Newell noticed Ernest staring at him. "What the hell are *you* looking at?" Newell barked as he raised a spoonful of cereal to his mouth.

"Your face! You're starting to look like a derelict, and we'll be going to Millie's tomorrow. Don't you care what people will think?" Ernest asked, bracing himself for the wrath to come.

Newell put down his spoon, and said, slowly, "Number one: No, I don't give a damn what people will think. And number two: I don't care what *you* think either, *and,* for your information, I've decided to grow a beard."

"A beard?! Why in the world do you want to grow a beard now, at your age?!" Newell fingered the hairs on his chin and said, "Well, Tyrone Power had a beard, and he was a very handsome man in his day. I think I could look a little bit like him if I had some facial hair."

Ernest stifled a laugh and said, "And who might you want to look handsome *for*, brother? Gracie? Millie? GERT?!"

"Oh, you think you're so funny. I'll have you know that I had quite a few young ladies seeking my company back in the day when I played for the Chargers. I had to fight 'em off!"

"Well, that was then, and this is now, and I haven't seen any ladies beating down your door lately!" Ernest said, chuckling.

Newell just let that comment slide and carefully stepped outside on the side stair landing to get a breath of fresh air and let his anger subside.

The next day they walked into Millie's. Ernest hung up their coats, and they were met with furtive glances and low whispers as they made their way to a booth.

Newell looked, for all the world, like a character out of a movie, and that character was *not* played by Tyrone Power. Newell was oblivious to the stir, but Ernest was a little embarrassed because he knew that people would think he wasn't taking good care of his older brother. Six-days growth was looking pretty bad.

"Poor old Newell," Frances Calderone said to her sister Helene as she was trying to pry the top off the packet of strawberry jam. "Now he's all alone."

"He has Ernest," Helene replied.

"Oh, it's not the same and you know it. He and Catherine were crazy about each other, and you know, with no kids and all, it must be hard."

Helene said, "Well, there's a reason that phrase is in the wedding vows: 'til death do us part.' It's just to be expected at that age. One will lose the other. No way around it," and she took the jam from her sister and opened it for her.

The brothers ordered their lunch, and, as he was handing his menu back to Gracie, Newell noticed Polly Grant sitting across the restaurant near the door with a woman he didn't know, and she seemed to be staring at him. He cleared his throat, and sat up a little taller in his seat.

He tried not to be obvious, but every time he looked over, Polly was squinting her eyes and smiling. He was convinced that his new look was the reason. He felt downright debonair. He smiled widely at her, gave her a little wave, and ran his fingers through his hair on one side.

They finished their lunch and got up to leave. As they neared the door, Newell said, "Well, hello there, Polly!" with a flourish.

Polly looked up, a bit startled, and said, "Oh, hello, Newell! Hello, Ernest! I didn't know you were here! This is my sister, Mabel. She's visiting all the way from Toronto!"

They all said polite hellos.

Polly said, "Don't you love Millie's homemade cinnamon raisin bread? And her specials are always so reasonable! I just wish she would print them on a piece of paper instead of putting them up on the chalkboard over there behind the booths. I can't even read them!"

Deflated, Newell said, "Well, nice to see you, Polly. Nice to meet you, Mabel," and walked out on the arm of Ernest, scratching the scraggy hair on his cheek.

Undaunted, he kept growing his so-called beard, and the longer it got, the worse he was looking.

"Meu Deus!" Isabella yelled when Newell came through the kitchen door the following Tuesday. She hadn't seen him in two weeks, and his beard shocked her.

"You look like a goat!" she exclaimed, realizing immediately how that must have sounded.

He had a pained look on his face, and she stammered, "Oh, Mr. Newell, I, I don't mean to insult you! I *love* my goats, and I love their little beards! You just reminded me of my little Pedro!" She sheepishly scooted past him and disappeared into the bathroom to start her cleaning.

That night after dinner, Ernest said, "Sooo, Isabella thinks you look like an old goat!" And he started laughing, and continued to laugh even though he saw that Newell was getting mad.

They went to bed without saying goodnight.

The next morning, Newell came into the kitchen clean-shaven – no trace of the beard, just a small Band-Aid on his cheek. Before Ernest could say anything, Newell put his hand up and said, "The damn beard was itchy as hell, okay?! And Tyrone Power looked handsome *without* a beard, too!"

Ernest was relieved that that little bump in the road was over, and life went on, uneventfully, for the most part.

Every now and then, Newell would feel for the hair on his face. Although he would never admit it, he was a little relieved that it was gone, too.

'*Maybe just a mustache…*'

Missing Cat

One evening, just as Newell had turned off the light and settled into bed, he felt Max jump up and nuzzle his face. "Well, hello there, my little furry friend! To what do I owe the honor of your company?"

She circled several times and plopped down next to his hip. You could always tell when a cat was going to stay put, because they took in a little breath and sighed. And she did.

This visit was quite unusual, because Max had slept with Ernest from the very first night she came on the scene. Newell didn't question it. He just sighed himself and fell asleep, with one hand gently on her back.

Newell loved this cat. She wasn't aloof like many cats can be. She was very affectionate, and, even though every piece of furniture in the house had claw marks on it, and she had batted two of Catherine's much-loved Hummel figurines off the fireplace mantle, shattering them to pieces, he loved having her around.

There were two flower beds on the property: The pansy and annual bed in front, next to the driveway, and a good-sized perennial garden in the back yard. Weeding had become difficult for Ernest. He needed help.

"I'm going to the hardware store for some batteries and to see if I can find someone to help out with the weeding. Can you think of anything we need?" he said to Newell one morning.

"Yeah, WD-40. My bedroom door squeaks, and it drives me nuts."

"I think we have some in the basement, but I'll pick some up anyway," Ernest said. "I don't feel like going down there. Too many spider webs. Ugh, they give me serious creeps."

At Dave's Hardware, he asked Gary, the clerk at the counter, if he knew of anybody who could do some weeding. "Not off the top of my head, Ernest, but check the bulletin board over by the key machine. People leave their business cards and you might find someone there."

Ernest walked over to the board and his stomach churned. Tacked to it was a small poster with a picture of a cat on it.

MISSING CAT
"Smokey"
Female Tabby.
Cash reward.

The cat looked exactly like Max. His heart was beating fast as he walked back over to Gary and asked, trying not to sound panicky, "Hey, Gary, how long has that cat poster been there?"

"Oh, quite a while. At least a year, I'd say. I should probably take it down," he answered.

Ernest went back over to the poster and saw that there was a phone number. He didn't know what to do. He stood there, feeling numb for a few moments. Finally, he took a deep breath, went back over to Gary and asked if he had a piece of paper and a pen. Gary handed him a slip of paper and a pencil, and Ernest went back and wrote down the phone number. He walked out to the car, got in and just sat there, staring out the windshield, feeling a little queasy.

'*What if it's Max?!*'

He couldn't stand this cat when she first entered their lives. Everything she did drove him crazy. But, now that he thought about it and pictured her gone, he realized that he really cared for this animal. Swallowing hard, he started thinking of valid reasons to let her go:

The expense: Her food, litter, vet bills, and even the damn tuna that Newell snuck home from the market, all added up. Having a pet was expensive.

The hassle: Emptying her litter box was a chore he hated. Cleaning up hairball-vomit made him gag every time. Every single time.

Cat hair: It was everywhere. Even though Isabella kept the house very clean, nothing could prevent Max from shedding, and every couple of days he had to use one of those sticky roller things to remove the hair from his clothes and the furniture. Once, he even tried using it on Max, but she bolted off his lap with a snarl.

It was no use. He couldn't bear the thought of letting her go. And suddenly, he thought of Newell! How could he tell Newell that they might have to give Max back to her rightful owners? He drove home slowly, his head spinning, pondering this unsettling turn of events.

'Well, they'll never have to know, will they? And so much time has passed, that they probably think she was hit by a car and stopped looking for her. They probably forgot the poster was even there!'

As hard as he tried to justify keeping her, his conscience prevailed, and he knew he had to call the number on the poster. He wouldn't tell Newell just yet.

A few days later, on a particularly nice afternoon, Ernest said, "Newell, why don't you sit outside and get some fresh air? It's a beautiful day! I have a couple of chores to finish up, but I'll join you in a few minutes."

Newell agreed, grabbed his cane, crossword puzzle book and a pencil, and went outside. He sat in one of the two lawn chairs that were set up on the right side of the house and was happy to feel the warmth of the sun on his shoulders.

His heart pounding, Ernest picked up the phone and dialed the number that was on the poster. He heard, one – two – three rings, and then a message:

'The number you are calling has been changed. The new number is 555-12...'

He hung up. It was an unfamiliar area code.

"They must have moved!" he said. "Okay, well, I tried."

He stared at the phone for several minutes, pacing back and forth. He peeked out the window and saw that Newell was still sitting in the sun, doing his puzzle. Frowning, and with hesitant resolve, he picked up the phone again, dialed the original number, and listened to the message. He wrote down the new number. His guilt had gotten the best of him, and he, with a pained heart, was about to call the person who just might be the original owner of their beloved Max.

The phone rang three times, and he nearly hung up, but then heard, "Hello?"

He hesitated, and a woman's voice said, "Hello? Hello? Is anyone there?"

"Hello. My name is Ernest Madison. I saw your poster at Dave's Hardware and was wondering if you were still missing a cat?" He had his fingers crossed, silently hoping she would say no.

There was a brief silence on the other end, and then he heard her gasp. Finally, she said, "Oh, my goodness, yes! Have you seen Smokey?!"

His heart sank. He said, "Well, maybe. My brother and I took in a stray quite a while ago. She was in pretty bad shape, but she's fine now."

"Oh, my poor baby! You see, we moved, and while we were packing, she got into one of the packing crates. You know, cats and boxes! It was put onto the moving van, and on route to our new house, the movers had to make a stop to shift the load, and one of them heard her mewing from inside the box. When he opened it, she got spooked, jumped out, and ran off. They tried to find her but gave up because they had a schedule to meet. Our family was heartbroken! Thank you so much for calling! We're only an hour and a half away in Parkerville, so I can come and pick her up whenever it's convenient for you! Just give me your address. Oh, this is such good news!"

Ernest felt lightheaded. After a long pause, he said, "Okay, yes, yes, that will be fine." He gave her their address and said, "Um, I just want you to know that we have really come to care for Max…sorry, *Smokey*. Especially my older brother, Newell. She's been really good for him, and he loves her. We have taken very good care of her, and she seems very happy here, but I understand. She is your cat."

He almost choked on the words.

"Ernest, Dear Ernest, I can come next Wednesday, at noon, if that works for you," she said with giddiness in her voice.

Trying to gather his thoughts, he said, "Okay, then. I'm very happy that you will be reunited. See you Wednesday," he said, his voice cracking.

He hung up the phone and sat down at the kitchen table. He put his head in his hands and wondered how he was going to break it to Newell. Just then, Max came into the room and jumped up on the table. She walked right up to him, nuzzled his face, and looked right into his eyes as if she knew something serious was going on.

Wednesday came fast. Ernest hadn't had the heart to tell Newell about the situation, and before he knew it, a car pulled up and parked at the curb on the street. Newell was outside, sitting on one of the lawn chairs, his head nodding, sound asleep. Ernest hurried down to the car as a woman was getting out.

"Hello, I'm Connie, Smokey's owner."

"Hello, Connie, I'm Ernest. And that's my brother, Newell, up there in the yard."

Connie looked up at Newell, and said, "Oh, he's quite old, isn't he? I can see how a cat is a comfort. And you said he really loves Smokey, didn't you?"

"We BOTH do!" he said, choking back a tear.

"Well, Ernest, I've been thinking about this. I didn't have your number or I would have called you. My kids were devastated after Smokey disappeared, so a couple of months after we lost her, we got another cat from our local shelter. She is gray, as well, and we decided to name her Smokey II. The kids love her, and they seem to have forgotten about our first Smokey. Also, to tell you the truth, I am quite sure our cat would not be happy with a strange cat in the house. They are quite territorial, you know. And I can see that my baby has a good home now. I think it would be best if you kept her."

Ernest had all he could do to keep from hugging her, but he stifled his joy as she continued,

"…And, as much as I would like to see her and hold her, I'm afraid it would confuse her, and it would break my heart, so I will just go. Ernest, I truly appreciate your contacting me. It was a very caring thing to do. Take care, now."

And, with that, she got in her car and drove away.

Ernest just stood there and watched as she turned the corner at the end of the street.

Newell woke up as the car drove away. He saw Ernest at the end of the driveway and yelled down to him, "Who was that?"

"Just someone asking for directions, Newell. Let's go in. Time to feed the cat."

Pa rum pum pum pum

"Do you think you might want to put up a Christmas tree this year?" Ernest asked, knowing that this could be a delicate subject.

"Absolutely not! I'm done with Christmas!" Newell said, turning the page of the newspaper he was reading, so hard that it ripped.

Since Catherine passed there was no mention of Christmas in the house. She had loved the holiday and thoroughly enjoyed and celebrated everything about it. She decorated their home with fresh boughs of pine, both inside and out. Sparkling with tiny white lights, they graced the staircase railing and fireplace mantle. When the rooms were dim, it was a lovely sight. She set up a ceramic crèche scene on the piano, and she played Christmas songs from Thanksgiving right through New Year's Eve. When she wasn't playing, she had the radio tuned to the station dedicated to Christmas music.

They always had a freshly-cut tree decorated with beautiful glass ornaments and silver icicles, which she would hang carefully, just a few pieces at a time, so the strands glistened as they reflected the multicolored bulbs. Now, Newell had no interest in decorating the house, knowing that it would open a wound, evoking bittersweet memories.

Ernest hesitated, and then said, "Did you ever think that *I* might want to experience Christmas here? That *I* might want a tree?"

"It's my house, dammit!" Newell growled, instantly regretting the tone in which he said it. He knew he had hurt Ernest, but he was firm in his conviction that Christmas was something in his past, not to be celebrated, ever again, in this house. It was just too painful.

Ernest *loved* Christmas. He remembered, as a child, trying to hear

Santa Claus and his reindeer on the roof on Christmas Eve – getting up early, before everyone else on Christmas morning, and sneaking down the stairs to peek at the treasures that awaited him. The excitement, the sheer joy of opening gifts from Santa was always a thrill, and he loved it, and his very favorite Christmas song was 'The Little Drummer Boy.'

Even though they had a several-year difference in age, they always shared their Christmas gifts, at least for a couple of weeks. One year, one of Ernest's gifts was a Lionel Train set, and their parents set up the tracks around the base of the Christmas tree. Pushing a lever on the transformer blew the whistle, and there was a pellet that was put in the engine's smokestack, so as the train traveled around the track, puffy white smoke realistically billowed out. Every boy dreamed of having one, and the brothers played with it for hours on end.

Also under the tree were Erector sets, Lincoln Logs, and soldier figurines that would occupy them right up until bedtime. Ernest collected baseball cards, and his stocking was always filled with packs of cards in bubble gum wrappers. The dusty pink gum lost its flavor within minutes, but the cards were the real prize. Christmas was simply magical to the boy. He always dreaded New Year's Day because it meant the end of Christmas, or, as he called it, "The bestest holiday!"

Ernest dropped Newell off at Sal's for a haircut one morning and drove over to Hoffman's Department Store. He went to the Christmas section and bought himself a small, two-foot table-top Christmas tree decorated with colored lights and little gold and silver ball ornaments. He put it in the trunk of the car and waited until Newell was in bed that night to bring it in. He set it up on the bureau in his bedroom, behind the door. When Isabella came to clean, Ernest took her aside and asked her not to mention the tree to Newell. She looked puzzled, but agreed to keep his secret.

The brothers were having lunch at Millie's on a cold mid-December day, and Ernest got up to go to the restroom. A precocious six-year-old girl, sitting in a nearby booth with her mother, had been watching the brothers eating their meals in silence, not a word between them. In kindergarten, her class had made Christmas ornaments out of pipe-cleaners, and she had a few of them in her coat pocket. She noticed that Newell was frowning, and she thought he looked sad, so when she saw Ernest leave the booth, she walked over and handed Newell a little green ornament shaped like a Christmas tree with a red star at the top. "Merry Christmas, Mister!" she said, and ran back to her mother who was smiling at her sweet gesture.

Newell looked down at the wonky little tree and was touched by the girl's kindness. He smiled at her in acknowledgement, bowing his head and patting his heart with his hand. It suddenly occurred to him how selfish he had been in denying Ernest his Christmas. His brother had been very good to him and he really had not shown much, if any, appreciation. As Ernest was returning to the booth, Newell was trying to think how he could right his wrong.

Later that evening, he remembered that he had won the football pool at the barbershop a couple of months ago, and had put the money in his wallet and forgotten about it.

The next day, while Ernest was outside clearing the car of a sheet of ice that had formed overnight, Newell called Sal at the barbershop.

"Hey, Sal, I'd like to surprise Ernest with a Christmas tree, but I don't know how to go about getting it here. Any chance you could pick one up for me, an artificial one is fine. I don't want to trouble you, and I'll pay you when you come? He has a dentist appointment on the 14th at 10:30, so that would be a good time to bring it over. I'd really appreciate it. He deserves better than I've been dishing out."

"Oh, Newts, that's a nice idea you got there," Sal replied. "I'll be working, but I'll ask a couple of the guys. It won't be a problem."

The day came, and two regulars from the barbershop, Al and Darnell, pulled up in a pickup truck at 10:45. They knew Newell didn't have a lot of money, so rather than buy an artificial tree which would have been quite expensive, they stopped at the Rotary Club display and picked up a 5 1/2-foot balsam fir. Sal had extra strings of lights and a tree stand in his back room, and gave them to the men to bring over.

In no time, they had the tree set up in the living room and strung the lights. Darnell plugged it in, and when Newell saw the tree lit up, he became emotional, but he kept it together until the guys left. He sat down in his chair, gazing at the tree, and his mind was flooded with years of Christmas memories with his dear Catherine. But, suddenly, instead of feeling mournful, a wave of gratitude washed over him. He had spent most of his life with a wonderful woman, and he realized he was incredibly blessed to have such precious memories to cherish. Many had not been so lucky – like his own brother.

There were no ornaments, and he certainly couldn't go down the cellar stairs to bring them up, but he remembered the pipe-cleaner ornament the little girl had given him. He went and got it out of his coat pocket and hung it on the tree near the top.

About an hour later Ernest came home and was immediately hit with the evergreen fragrance of the fir. "What the…?" He walked into the living room and gasped when he saw the beautiful tree. "What's this?!" he said, walking over and touching the spiny needles. "Newell, what have you done?!"

"Merry Christmas, Ernest," Newell choked out, and, for the first time in their adult lives, the brothers hugged – an awkward but heartfelt embrace.

Just then, they heard a noise behind them and turned around to see Max, a third of the way up the tree trunk, peering out at them, and they both burst into laughter.

Newell walked over to the radio and tuned it to the Christmas station. The song that was playing was 'The Little Drummer Boy.'
A sweet gift of Christmas magic, custom-made for Ernest.
The ox and lamb kept time, pa rum pum pum pum…'
Sometimes in life, timing is everything.

71

Busted

"Newell…" Ernest said one afternoon, "Someday you'll have to tell me the story of when you took the car and went for a little joy ride."

Newell looked at him incredulously and said, "How did you know?!"

Ernest said, "Well, first I saw the pansy bed with the tire track through it. Then I was at the nursery, picking up some flowers to replace the ones you drove over, and I ran into Gert Stimpson. She couldn't wait to tell me that she had seen you driving *alone* near the bakery. *And,* I saw Billy Connors at the gas station, and he said Sergeant Earl told him he saw you driving *very* slowly up our street and pulling into the driveway. Billy was pretty perturbed but decided to let it go. Any way you look at it, Newell, you're busted."

"Why didn't you ever mention it?! Why didn't you yell at me?!"

"Well, I figured you must've had a darn good reason, and no harm was done, other than the pansies, so I let it lie."

"Thank you, Ernest," he said, gratefully. Ernest got up and patted him on the back as he went into the living room. It was time for his soap opera.

Newell was vastly relieved that he got away with his risky adventure unscathed. But he was especially grateful for Ernest's restraint and understanding. It was all so new.

He sat down at the table in the kitchen and started a crossword puzzle. Max jumped up, bumped his head with hers, and plopped down, right in the middle of the puzzle. Newell just smiled and began kneading her ears and neck, enjoying the soothing sound of her purring.

As he sat there, he entertained the thought of taking the car out again for a Dairy Queen someday.

"Nope," he said out loud. "Lesson learned."

And he could've sworn that Max nodded her head in agreement.

A Test of Courage

"Hey, did you pick up some WD-40 at Dave's? That damn squeak is really getting on my nerves," Newell said as they were finishing breakfast one morning.

"Oh, um, no. I got to talking to Gary, and it slipped my mind." Ernest felt his stomach turn when he remembered seeing the missing cat sign at the hardware store and thought about how close they came to losing Max.

Newell said, "Well, you said we had some in the cellar. Can you run down and get it?"

"Uh, okay, I'll go a little later on," Ernest said with a sinking feeling.

Even after all the rigorous training and the years of actual combat that Ernest faced while in the service, many times having to dig deep for courage, he was crippled by a life-long curse: Arachnophobia, an abject fear of spiders. He had only been down to the basement once, shortly after he moved in, and it rattled him so much that he vowed never to go down there again.

The cellar floor was half concrete and half dirt. The walls, except for one made up of small boulders fastened in place by cement, were dark gray plaster over cement, and the whole space was damp and dark, and there was a faint smell of mildew in the air. The only light shone in weakly from a far window in the back corner. There wasn't much stored down there, just old window screens, some rusted garden tools, and the long-neglected Christmas decorations. There was a workbench with bins of screws, nails, and tools collecting dust, because it had been years since Newell had been able to do any kind of projects.

And there were spiders…lots and lots of spiders, their carefully spun webs decorating the space like something out of a Halloween haunted house or a horror movie.

He put it off until the afternoon, and then considered the situation. He was tempted to just drive over to Dave's and pick up a new can of lubricant, but he shook that idea off and, feeling a shiver run up his spine, decided to tough it out. He knew his was an irrational fear, as most phobias are, but still, his aversion was real.

He grabbed the flashlight from the drawer and got the broom out of the closet to use for clearing his path. He opened the cellar door, which was right off the hall, feeling just as apprehensive as he had on the first day of boot camp.

"Okay, here I go," he said to himself, trying to bolster his courage. *"They're just little spiders, for heaven's sake!"*

The stairs were steep, so he had to be careful as he held the broom in front of him with his right hand, waving it back-and-forth as if he was in a dueling battle with a fearsome foe, which, in his mind, he *was*. He couldn't use the railing because he had the flashlight in his other hand, and he was relieved when he finally made it down. He shivered with revulsion as the flashlight illuminated his worst nightmare: dozens of spiderwebs blocking his path to the work bench where the WD-40 sat, as if taunting him, saying, *"Heh, heh, heh, come and get me, Errrnest."*

He flailed around with the broom, which was becoming covered with the sticky silken webs, and finally he took a deep breath, hurried over to the bench, and grabbed the can, just as a large dark spider crawled up his arm.

"Agghh! Son of a bitch!" he yelled as he shook his arm until the thing fell off.

Just then, he heard a rustling noise in the far corner of the cellar. His nerves were already shot, so this really shook him up. Suddenly, he felt like a child who had taken a bad spill off his bike and skinned his knee. He needed his mother to kiss it and make it better.

He was not about to investigate the source of the noise, and he hurried back over to the stairs and started back up. When he saw that the broom was wrapped like a cocoon in webs and spiders he threw it back down, his heart beating wildly. He burst into the living room, his eyes wide, and he was breathing heavily.

Newell was sitting in his chair stroking Max and asked, "You okay? You look like you've seen a ghost!"

"Here's your damn WD-40! I'm *fine!*" He tossed the can to Newell and went to the closet for the whisk broom to brush off the spider webs that had stuck to his hair and clothes. He didn't realize it, but he had left the cellar door ajar, and Max, hearing the scratching noise from the cellar, jumped off of Newell's lap and headed for the door.

"No, no, no, NO!" Ernest yelled as he saw her disappear down the stairs. Now he had a real dilemma. His choices were to leave the door open and wait for Max to come back up, knowing that the open door could allow access to the spiders, ("*which will come into my bedroom and crawl on my bed and…*"), or go back down and bring Max up with him. He quickly nixed the second option, wincing at the thought.

"We must have a mouse," he said to Newell, his voice shaking.

"Yeah, we used to get them every now and then," Newell said. "There should be some traps down there if Max doesn't get him."

Ernest tried calling Max, but she wouldn't come back up. She was in a crouched position in front of the boiler, poised to pounce on whatever critter was lurking there. Her very own boot camp. She was on patrol.

Half an hour went by, and Ernest tried to distract himself by reading his book. His skin crawled at the thought of Max coming back up, covered with spiderwebs. He said, "I'm going for a ride. I'll be back in a little while," and strode into the kitchen and out the door as Newell scratched his head, wondering what the heck was going on.

He just drove around, glad to be out of the house and away from the damn spiders, but it was getting near dinner time so he knew he had to get back. Just to kill some more time, he swung over to Bruno's Pizza in the Italian section of town and ordered a small half-cheese and half-mushroom pie to go.

Newell was standing in front of the refrigerator with the freezer door open as Ernest came through the kitchen door. Max was sitting on the counter licking her front paw.

"She brought me a little present," Newell said, as he put something small wrapped in foil into the freezer and shut the door.

"A mouse? Did you shut the cellar door!?"

"I did," Newell replied. "Maxie looked pretty proud of herself when she dropped the little sucker at my feet."

"Was she covered with spider webs?" Ernest asked, opening the pizza box.

"No, she was fine. You'd better set a couple of traps down there tomorrow. There could be a family of mice," Newell said, as he took two plates out of the cabinet.

"Oh, I don't *think* so! No need! We have a mouser!" and he took the cat's face in both hands and kissed the top of her head. Then he went into the hall and opened the cellar door, just a crack, for Max. He knew he could deal with one spider now and then, as long as he never had to go down to that dreaded chamber of horrors again.

"Man, I love pizza!" Newell said, taking a bite. "Hey, you don't like spiders, do you, brother?"

"Where'd you get that idea?" Ernest said, reaching for a slice of pizza, and *really* hoping that Newell wouldn't notice his head-to-toe, full-body shudder. Casually, he said, "By the way, we'll need a new broom."

In bed that night, Ernest thought to himself: *"Man, I deserve a medal!"* and he wondered how he would ever fall asleep, re-living his valiant and hard-fought battle with his tiny fearsome foes.

Time Has Wings

"Do you want to know what's wrong with getting old, Ernest? We don't have *experiences*."

"What do you mean by experiences?" Ernest said, curious as to where this was going.

"Experiences are when you travel, or go dancing, or water skiing, or go on a trail hike, or go white water rafting. You know, things like that."

"Well, we are pretty limited as to what we can do, Newell. Do you have anything in mind?"

"No, I don't. It just seems that one day flows into the next, with nothing really happening, nothing to look forward to. The damn kitchen clock with its incessant 'tick-tock, tick-tock' reminds me that life is speeding by, and I don't experience anything that gets my juices flowing!

"You know what, Ernest? I'm not afraid of dying. I'm afraid of not *living!* Catherine and I used to go dancing all the time. We loved it! Now, I can't even *walk*, dammit!"

Then he said, "You know that old saying, 'Life is like a roll of toilet paper: The closer you get to the end – the faster it goes'? Well, there's a lot of truth to that!"

Ernest was silent, taking in what his brother was trying to express.

Newell went on: "Do you remember when Satchel Paige asked, 'How old would you be if you didn't know how old you are?'"

Ernest nodded.

79

Sitting forward in his chair, Newell asked, "How old would *you* be, Ernest?"

"Oh, probably around sixty, I guess," he replied.

"Well, I'm thirty-five. Yep, I stopped there, and, in my head, I will be thirty-five until the day I die."

He continued. "Young people think old people have old minds, old thoughts. Hell, not even young people! *Fifty-year-olds* are worried about aging because they think that once your skin is wrinkled, that your mind stops being lively, that you only think about *old* people's things. Sure, some people get dementia and literally lose their minds, lose themselves, but most of us, our geriatric-selves, have the *same* passions, the *same* interest in life that we did when we were decades younger. Damn, I hate the word *elderly!*"

Ernest knew he was right, but he didn't know how to liven things up in their lives.

He thought about it over the next few weeks, and one afternoon, like the distant tinkling of a neighbor's porch chime, the idea landed softly in his mind. Every summer, there was an Italian Heritage Festival downtown, along the river. They had never gone to it, but it was a very popular event and everyone had great things to say about it. There was music, dancing, lots of wonderful food, and a lively procession honoring an Italian saint that wound its way through the throngs of people who were there celebrating.

Ernest had a mission: To get Newell to this festival. It wouldn't be easy.

A Little Opera

The brothers were due for a haircut. They went about every six or seven weeks, no set schedule. Ernest didn't have much on top, but Newell had a full head of pure white hair, and when it got long, he thought it made him look older.

"Ernest, it's time to go to Sal's."

Sal's was an old-fashioned barbershop located downtown just up the block from Bruno's. It was a neighborhood hangout where guys could get a shave and a haircut and spend a couple of hours talking sports, reading the newspaper, catching up on local gossip, having a cup of coffee or an espresso (with a shot of Sambuca if they liked), or sitting in on a card game in the back room.

Newell used an adjustable razor at home, but Ernest preferred to use an electric razor, so he would skip the shave, get his haircut first, and then leave Newell there while he did errands or stopped in to the bookstore on White Avenue. He would pick up used copies of westerns or mystery novels for himself and crossword books for Newell. They both enjoyed the time away from each other, and Newell always looked forward to the pampered treatment he got from Sal.

Salvatore Damiani had come over from the old country to follow in his father's and grandfather's footsteps in the business. Barbers needed

81

to be licensed, and he learned the ropes at barber school back in Naples. He had three chairs – big, beautiful, impressive chairs with black leather and chrome. He wasn't a 'spaccone.' He didn't brag, but he was very proud of them because they symbolized his success in the new country. The shop's walls were covered with sports memorabilia, pin-up girls cut out from men's magazines, a picture of the Pope (carefully positioned so as not to face the sexy pictures), and a photo of Enrico Caruso, the famous Italian tenor, another Napolitano, whose amazing voice lent a true Italian vibe to the shop from the record player near the window. This place had *atmosphere*.

There were several small, straight-backed chairs around the room in case there was a wait for a shave. Sal did a brisk business, and no one minded waiting. There were milk crates here and there on the floor filled with magazines: *Sports Illustrated*, *Popular Mechanics*, *Men's Digest*, and some store catalogs and comic books.

Early every morning, Sal's wife, Evelina, made Biscotti and Italian Knot Cookies: soft almond confections with vanilla icing and pastel sprinkles on top that melted in your mouth. Sal kept a basket filled with them on a side table. They were really good with the coffee.

Today there were five regulars in the shop, not including Newell, and a few in the back – some, no doubt, losing their shirts in a poker game. Everybody knew everybody. A lot of the guys had nicknames left over from school or the service:

Pete, 'Tank,' was once a middle-weight amateur boxer and had the nose to prove it. Walter, 'Walleye,' was an avid fisherman. Frank, 'Grease,' owned an auto repair shop in town. Darnell, 'Tats,' was a Marine vet who was used to good-natured ribbing for getting tattoos in the service, even though his skin was very dark, and Al, 'Boner,' because he had a bad comb-over, was short, round, and looked a bit like Napoleon Bonaparte.

Newell waited while Ernest got his haircut and then was helped up into the middle chair by Ernest and Sal. He settled his feet on the padded footrest, and smiled, anticipating a nice time and a great shave.

"See you in a couple," Ernest said as he left the shop, and the shave began.

Sal draped a black cape around Newell's shoulders, placed a piping-hot towel on his face, and walked to another chair. Newell closed his eyes and sat back and listened as the conversation in the shop touched on local and federal politics, the latest baseball trades and game scores, and what had happened on various TV shows the night before.

Nearly every day, Sal couldn't resist telling the story of the barber pole:

"Hey, you guys, listen to this! This is *unbelievable!* In the old, the *really* old days, they used to drain blood from people for their health. They called it *bloodletting!* Sometimes they even used *leeches*! Ecchh!"

He would look around for a reaction, then continue: "The red on the barber pole represents for blood, and the white means for the bandages they used! And, go figure, nobody really knows what the blue is for! And, the pole, itself, represents for the stick the patient squeezed to get the vein to pop up! Aaghh! Mamma Mia!"

Sal held the leather strop straight out from a hook on the chair and sharpened his straight razor while he asked how Newell was doing. Regardless of how many shaves one has had, there was always a little bit of nervousness when that razor came out, especially when it came near your throat. Of course, no one would ever admit it.

Sal removed the still-hot towel and slathered Newell's face with a luxurious shaving cream, using a round natural-bristle brush. Then he began shaving with confident strokes, starting at the sideburns and working downward. He was humming along with Caruso singing

83

'*Santa Lucia*' but stopped when he noticed a small scab on Newell's cheek.

"Questo? What's this?" he asked, holding the razor in the air, waiting for an answer.

"Oh, hell, I decided to grow a beard a while back, but I lost patience with it, and I nicked myself trying to shave it off," he replied, feeling a bit embarrassed. "I don't have your finer talents," he said winking at Sal.

"That's why I get the bigga bucks!" Sal said, and they both laughed. There was a warm affection between them.

When the shave was over, Sal put a bracingly-cold towel on Newell's face to tighten his pores and left him to work on another customer. He returned in a few minutes, removed the towel, and slapped some strongly scented astringent aftershave on Newell's face. It was a great ending to a great shave.

Then came the haircut: He used scissors because of the length of Newell's hair. He had an unruly cowlick that refused to cooperate, so Sal just cut it close to his scalp. He used electric clippers to trim the back of his neck, and when he finished the cut, he carefully snipped the hair out of his nostrils and ears. All the loose hair was knocked off his neck and shoulders with a large, soft-bristled brush. When he was finished, Sal removed the cape, and helped Newell down to a side chair to wait for Ernest.

He said, "Hey, Newts, you got something wrong with your legs, or they just weak?"

Newell said, "Just weak is all. I don't exercise, not since Catherine passed, so they're like your dinner last night – spaghetti."

"Take a look at this," Sal said, reaching for a catalog in a bin and opening it up to a dog-eared page. "It's a pedal exercising thing. You sit down and use your legs like on a bicycle while you're watching TV. My buddy Gennaro bought one for his uncle Vincenzo who couldn't walk, like you, and he threw his walker away after a couple months! You should try it."

Newell shook his head, and said, "Nah, I'm too old for that. Too late for me."

Tank overheard their conversation and said, "Hey, I just read about an old guy, a ninety-year-old guy, who just ran a *marathon*. They interviewed him in a magazine, and you know what he said?"

They both shook their heads, waiting for his answer.

"This old bastard said he didn't start running until he was sixty-seven, and they quoted him as saying: 'Oh, to be seventy again!' How do you like that!?"

Newell had a flashback of himself falling at home, and his stomach turned over. He put his hand out, and Sal passed the catalog to him. Ernest came through the door just then and, after grabbing a few cookies and saying goodbye to Sal and the guys, they left.

That night at the kitchen table after dinner, Newell slid the catalog over to Ernest and asked him to send away for the exercise machine. Without a word, Ernest took the catalog and nodded his head.

Newell got a clean shave that day, and possibly, he thought to himself, a new lease on life.

Pedal to the Metal

The doorbell rang, and by the time Ernest got there, a delivery man was on his way back to his truck, and a box was on the top step. He brought it in, relieved that it was pretty light because his back was kicking up. He put it down on the kitchen table, took a pair of scissors out of the drawer, and sliced through the packing tape.

Newell was in the living room and yelled, "Is that my bike?" knowing full well that it was because they rarely got parcel post deliveries.

Ernest brought the box into the living room and put it down on the coffee table. He opened the top and cursed when he saw that the box was full to the brim with Styrofoam peanuts. He hated those things. They were so light that they flew everywhere when taking the contents out of the box. He reached in and dozens of peanuts floated out and down onto the table and floor. He carefully tried to pull out the exercise gadget which was wrapped in clear plastic. As hard as he tried to avoid it, more peanuts landed on the floor. He finally gave up trying to be careful, yanked out the contraption, and by now the floor looked like a winter wonderland. Frustrated, he put the box on the floor and went to get the broom and dustpan. He came back and swept up all the peanuts and put them back in the box. It wasn't easy because they were so light that they just floated around when he tried to capture them with the broom.

He took the instruction manual out of its plastic sleeve and handed it to Newell, who had been silently watching, with a slight smile on his face.

Ernest went back to the closet to put the broom away just as Max came into the living room and spotted the box. Without the slightest hesitation, she took a four-foot flying leap and jumped right in, peanuts flying everywhere.

Newell burst out laughing. He couldn't hold it in anymore. This cat could do no wrong in his eyes, but when Ernest came back and saw what had happened, he blew a gasket. The floor was covered with peanuts again, and Max had jumped back out of the box and started batting them around. A few landed under the couch and this became a fun game for her. She would bat them under the couch and then try to retrieve them.

"Aagghh! Damn cat!" Ernest yelled, and headed back to the broom closet.

After the mess was all cleaned up and Ernest had calmed down, he examined the exerciser which was in several pieces: metal rods, screws, nuts, bolts, pedals, straps, and rubber feet, and cursed again because now he had to assemble the thing.

"Newell, you'd better use this damn thing! I'm not going through all this for nothing!"

Little did he know that Newell was more than ready to use 'this damn thing.' He had spent many nights in bed thinking about the possibility of strengthening his legs.

He hated the walker.

He hated the cane.

He hated depending on Ernest for every damn thing.

He was ready.

Ernest assembled the machine, which took a good thirty minutes, and put it down in front of Newell's feet. It was about a foot and a half wide and a little over a foot long. There were two rods with rubber feet on them connected by one arched rod in the middle where the pedal assembly was attached. Newell put one foot at a time on the pedals. They had adjustable straps, so Ernest made sure they fit comfortably around Newell's arches. He took a deep breath and started pedaling. There was no resistance at all. None.

"This thing is useless!" Newell yelled.

Ernest picked up the instruction booklet and saw that there was a tension adjustment knob. He gave it a couple of clicks and said, "Okay, try it again."

Newell tried to pedal, but his legs were too weak to push even one rotation.

"Try one click down," he said to Ernest.

He turned the tension down one click, and Newell started pedaling again.

"This feels just about right, Ernest. Watch me go!" as his feet went round and round.

Ernest said, "Whoa! Pull up on the reins, Buddy. You haven't used those muscles in *years*, and the *last* thing you need is to be laid-up in pain because you overdid it! Start with three minutes, and then you can work up from there."

Newell knew he was right. He could really set himself back if he was too eager.

"Take it slow, Newell. We can do this," he thought to himself.

No Cane, and Able

Ernest was impressed with Newell's dedication to his new exercise routine. He had started slowly, every other day, with the resistance on the machine set on two, and then slowly worked his way up, over the course of several weeks, until he was working at the highest resistance the machine would reach – five.

While pedaling, Newell would place his hands on the top of his thighs and feel his quadriceps working. His calves were getting stronger, too. The mental image of the ninety-year-old who ran the marathon kept him at it whenever he got tired and was tempted to quit or skip a few days. Willpower is a funny thing. You really needed incentive and motivation for it to kick in and Newell had both. He wanted to walk, unencumbered by the cane, his walker, or his brother. And he dreaded the thought of himself in a wheelchair or a motorized scooter, which he knew would be his fate if he didn't persevere.

Encouraged by his progress, he decided to take it a step further, so every time he stood at the sink to do the dishes, or in the bathroom to brush his teeth, he stood on one foot for as long as he could, with one hand on the counter, to work on his balance.

Within two months he was getting around much easier, his pain had subsided slightly, and he would test his strength by walking, cane in hand in case he needed it, from room to room. He could get up and out of his chair without a lot of effort, and even getting off the toilet was not as difficult as it used to be.

The real test would be going to Millie's for the first time without any support.

The big day came, and Newell said, "I'm good without the cane," as they were leaving the house.

"You sure?" Ernest asked as he walked around to the driver's side of the car. He knew Newell had gotten stronger just by watching him move around the house, but Millie's was a different story. There were steps to climb to get inside, and he didn't want Newell to be embarrassed in case he faltered.

"I'm sure," he said, and got in the car.

Ernest pulled up to the curb and went around to open Newell's door. He helped him out of the car as usual, but then Newell walked confidently across the sidewalk, up the three stairs, and right through the door of the restaurant.

The regulars noticed right away. Newell was standing taller and walking unaided. He was so pleased he could have burst, and it showed.

Gracie's eyes welled up when she saw him stride to the booth, and she elbowed Millie, alerting her to watch.

It was a real relief for Ernest, too. He had constantly worried about Newell falling, and that worry was gone now.

He didn't mention it, but Ernest would see to it that they went to the Italian Festival in July.

Newell would have his "EXPERIENCE."

The Funeral

Newell was in the bathroom when the phone rang. He couldn't hear the conversation, but he could tell Ernest was upset.

"Who called?" he asked, walking into the kitchen.

"Tank is gone," Ernest replied, his eyes wet and wide.

"What do you mean *gone?*" Newell said, as he sat down at the kitchen table across from his brother.

"Pete, Pete O'Brien is dead. Massive heart attack. There was no saving him. Margaret must be devastated!"

"Wow, he seemed fine the last time we saw him! Jeez, you just never know," Newell said, shaking his head. "We'll have to go to the services. *Damn*, I hate funerals!"

"Yes, of course we will. Remember how good they were to you when Catherine passed? Margaret brought over casseroles and pies, and Tank came over once a week to keep you company for the longest time."

Newell said, "You're right, they were wonderful. It's all a blur to me now, but I remember their kindness. I wish I could repay it somehow."

That night, Newell couldn't fall asleep. He kept thinking about Tank. He had met him at Sal's years ago, and they hit it off immediately. He had a great Irish sense of humor and always had a joke or two for the guys at the shop. Most of his jokes were off-color, but there were never ladies around, so it was okay. Tank couldn't tell a joke without laughing at it himself, which made them even funnier.

His nose was flattened, and he had a scar over his right eye, separating his eyebrow by half an inch – evidence of his boxing days. His build was muscular, short, and wide. It was hard to think of him dead. He had been so very full of life. As sleep neared, Newell was thinking of what he could possibly do for Margaret.

The brothers attended the wake and the funeral, and Newell hated every bit of it. It all reminded him of Catherine's services: The cloyingly-sweet smell of trumpet lilies and carnations in the funeral parlor, the doleful piped-in organ music in the background, the long lines of people paying their respects, and mourners sitting in rows of chairs, in polite, hushed conversation. He couldn't even bring himself to look at Tank in the coffin. That was the part he hated the most.

The last time they wore their suits was for Catherine's funeral, and they didn't realize that they didn't fit anymore because they both had gained weight from Isabella's cooking. Neither of their jackets would close, and they couldn't button the top button of their trousers.

"Well, at least the ties fit!" Newell said, laughing.

Ernest had an idea: They would wear V-neck sweaters under their suit coats, hiding the waist gap, solving the problem, and avoiding embarrassment. They actually looked quite presentable at the services.

"Well, I'm glad that's over. That was quite a turn-out for Tank, wasn't it?" Newell said to Ernest as he was reaching for a cookbook on the shelf in the kitchen a few days later.

"Um…what are you doing?" Ernest said, eyeing the cookbook.

"I had an idea is all," Newell said with a bit of an edge to his voice. "I want to make Catherine's chicken casserole for Margaret." Raising his hand, he said a bit defensively, "Ernest, I don't want to hear about it. *Don't* tell me I can't cook. I used to help her peel potatoes, and I have a pretty good idea of how she put it together. I just have to find her recipe and make a shopping list."

Ernest's first impulse was to talk him out of it because he knew it could turn into a disaster, but he decided to bite his tongue and let Newell attempt his kind deed.

"Let's see, it had chicken, potatoes, vegetables, and soup. Oh! cream of celery soup! That was her secret ingredient," Newell said as he flipped through the index in the cookbook. He looked at several different chicken recipes and couldn't find one that looked familiar. He took another cookbook down and, again, no luck. Then, he remembered Catherine's mother's recipe box. It was in an upper cabinet, in the back. It was red metal with whimsical kitchenware items painted on it. He placed it on the table and started thumbing through the cards.

"Bingo! Here it is! Creamy Chicken Casserole!" He pulled out a stained three-by-five index card and started writing the ingredients down on a pad of paper on the table.

"Are we going shopping tomorrow?" he asked Ernest, with a bit of urgency in his voice.

"Sure. We need milk, cereal, and cat food anyway," Ernest replied.

The next day at the market, the hunt for the recipe ingredients began.

"Three Russet potatoes. I think those are the big brown ones," Newell said, looking at his list. "One onion…here we go. It doesn't specify red or white. I'm going with white," Newell said, tossing a yellow onion into the cart. "Diced chicken – cooked. Hmm, I don't know about this, Ernest. Oh, wait, we could go to the deli and get a hunk of chicken and cut it up ourselves!"

"Ourselves?" Ernest said. "Does this mean I'm helping you?"

"Well, I might need a tiny bit of assistance. And besides, if this turns out okay, we might want to make one for us, too," Newell said with a little grin.

Ernest looked away, rolling his eyes.

"Okay, let's see here. One bag of frozen mixed vegetables, one can of cream of celery soup, one can of cream of chicken soup, eight ounces of cream cheese – room temperature, one can of chicken broth, salt, pepper – we have those, and one cup of shredded Cheddar cheese. French fried onions for the top. I think they come in a can," Newell said as he pushed the cart through the aisles.

They made their way through the market and found everything on the list.

"Oh, we should probably get one of those disposable aluminum casserole pans. That way Margaret won't have to return our dish," Ernest said, as they were heading to the checkout.

"Good idea, brother. This will be fun!" Newell chirped, smiling.

Ernest just sighed, picturing the kitchen after Newell got ahold of it.

The next morning, Ernest heard Newell in the kitchen. It was early: 6:45. He was rooting around in the utensil drawer for measuring spoons, a potato peeler, and a paring knife. Ernest decided to skip his shower and got dressed. He figured he'd better get in there before all hell broke loose. Newell's charitable venture could turn sour, fast.

"I remember Catherine said she measured everything first and had it ready before continuing with the recipe. She called it 'mice in plats,' or something like that, so that's what I'm doing," Newell said proudly as Ernest joined him at the counter. "I already chopped the chicken into chunks. I guess we're ready to go!" Newell said, excitedly.

"What do you want me to do?" Ernest asked, rolling up his sleeves.

"You can start opening the cans, and mash up the cream cheese with a fork. I took it out of the refrigerator earlier, so it should be soft enough."

Newell pulled the trash can over to the counter next to him, stepped on the pedal to open it, and started peeling the potatoes, dropping the skins into the open can. After only one potato, he said, "Ernest, I can't do this. My arthritis. Would you mind?"

Ernest hated that job, but he sighed, changed places with Newell, and began peeling the remaining potatoes.

There were three open cans on the counter: the two soups and one can of chicken broth. Newell grabbed a pair of scissors and began slicing open the frozen vegetables, but he lost his grip on the slippery bag and most of them fell into the sink and onto the counter, with the rest falling to the floor.

"Dammit!" he cried, as he tried to corral the corn, peas, and carrots into a pile in the sink. Max came sliding into the kitchen, sensing something interesting going on, and began eating the vegetables on the floor with abandon.

"Stop! Scoot, Max!" Ernest yelled, but the cat paid no attention. She was right under-foot, and Newell almost tripped over her as he reached for a big spoon to scoop up the vegetables in the sink.

Ernest went and got the dustpan and picked up whatever vegetables were left on the floor and threw them in the trash can. Just then, Max jumped up on the counter, every inch of which was covered with food, cans, and utensils, and she was quickly swept back down by Ernest.

"Stay down, Max!" he yelled, even though he knew that cats were deaf to commands of any kind. She hesitated for a few seconds, then jumped right back up on the other side of the sink, bumping one of the cans of soup and knocking it over. The cream of chicken soup oozed its way over to the recipe card and completely enveloped it before the brothers could react. Max flew off the counter, her paws dripping with soup.

"Oh, *NO!*" they both yelled, as they watched the ink on the card bleed into an illegible mess. Ernest quickly put the bowl with the vegetables under the lip of the counter, and guided the spilled soup into it with the side of his hand.

"Well, that was a bad start, wasn't it?" Newell said with a nervous laugh. "What do we do now?"

(If Ernest had enough hair to wring, he would be wringing it now).

"Well, dammit, we'll have to wing it! Catherine's recipe is ruined!" Ernest said at a near yell, as he peeled the onion and started chopping it, narrowly missing his fingers because his hands were shaking. He really wanted to keep his cool because Newell was on a charity mission, and he didn't want to dissuade him by showing his frustration. He took a few deep breaths and carried on.

"Do you remember what it said to do with the potatoes? Were they chopped or sliced?" he said, as Newell was rubbing the inside of the aluminum pan with Crisco.

"Sliced!" he said, happy to have remembered.

"Sliced *how?* Thick or thin?" Ernest said, again, trying hard not to sound exasperated.

"Well, everything here is pretty much cooked, so it probably won't take much time in the oven. I would slice them kind of thin, so they'll cook through."

"What about the cream cheese? What do we do with that?" Ernest said, as he dumped all the mixed vegetables, chicken, soups, broth, and onions into the pan.

"I don't know. Let's just mix it in. It's not like it's a fancy layered thing. It's just a casserole. It'll be just fine," Newell said with that nervous laugh again.

"What about the oven temperature? And how long, for heaven's sake?"

Newell picked up the recipe card and shook off the soup into the sink. He squinted at the card and the only thing he could make out was a five and a zero.

"Looks like five-hundred degrees," he said, and headed over to the oven to turn it on.

"No, no, NO! It can't be five-hundred degrees! That's too high! Hold your horses, for Criminy sake! Let me look at some chicken recipes in one of these cookbooks and see what the temperature is for something like this!" He took a cookbook from the shelf and found a chicken stew recipe which called for 350 degrees for forty-five minutes, covered with foil for the first half hour, then uncovered for the last fifteen minutes.

Ernest said, "Okay, let's cross our fingers and hope this works. Stir everything together and sprinkle the grated cheese on top. I don't know if the fried onions are supposed to go on now, or after it's cooked. What do you think?"

"I think they'd get soggy. Let's wait til the end," Newell said as he set the oven temperature.

"This place is a god-awful mess! You sit down, I'll clean up. You've been on your feet for quite a while now," Ernest said, beginning to wipe down the counter.

"You're a good brother, Ernest. Sorry I haven't told you that before. I, I, just got too wrapped up in my own…"

"Shhh. Enough of that talk. Let's get this thing in the oven and pray that we don't have to throw it in the trash!"

The timer went off after thirty minutes, and they both rushed into the kitchen from the living room to see what their creation looked like. Ernest held his breath as he opened the oven, pulled out the shelf with an oven mitt, and peeled off the foil. The casserole smelled wonderful, and it was bubbling, the chicken and potatoes starting to brown. He slid it back into the oven, and set the timer for fifteen minutes. "Well, if you go by the smell, this is going to be delicious!" Ernest said, sounding optimistic.

"This has been the longest forty-five minutes of my life!" Newell said as Ernest took the pan out of the oven at the end of the cooking time. The casserole was beautifully browned on top, the cheese was bubbling, and it smelled heavenly.

"I think we did it!" Ernest said, removing his oven mitts.

"We have to let it cool, add the fried onions, then later on we'll wrap it up, and take it over to Margaret."

"I'm pooped! How 'bout you?" Newell said as he sat down at the kitchen table, letting out a long exhale.

"Good grief, that was a workout, and a near disaster! I don't think Julia Child would approve of our technique, but I think she would be pleased with the results!" Ernest said, moving the trash can back to its place in the corner.

"Bon Appétit!" Newell chortled in a high-pitched voice, and they dissolved into exhausted laughter.

Later that afternoon, after calling to make sure it was a convenient time to go over, they delivered the casserole to Margaret. She thanked them profusely and invited them in, but they declined. She looked like she needed some rest, and they definitely needed some rest of their own.

About a week later, she called, and Newell answered the phone.

"Newell, it's Margaret. I want to thank you for bringing that delicious casserole over. It means so much to know that you care, and I know how much work it must have been for you! If you don't mind, could I possibly have the recipe?"

Newell said, "I'm so glad you enjoyed it, Margaret. I would love to give you the recipe, but, you see, I can't give away my Catherine's secret ingredient."

And he smiled into the afternoon, that night, and right into part of the next day. He felt really proud and happy to have been able to return her kindness.

"Heck, I could do that again, now that I know what I'm doing," he said to himself, and took a cookbook down from the shelf.

"Yessiree, I just might have myself a new hobby! Let's see here… Oh, meatloaf!"

Un-Conventional Geneva

As a girl, Geneva Conte was a real spark plug. She was funny, vivacious, gutsy, and a delight to be around. She had transferred from a school in another part of the state in the seventh grade. It was always difficult for students to assimilate into a new school environment, but her bubbly personality won her friends immediately. Soon after transferring, she joined several school organizations: the Glee Club; the Drama Club; the Library Service Club; and she was elected to be a cheerleader from eighth grade all the way through high school. She was voted Most Popular two years in a row, but it never went to her head.

Being a cheerleader was much like being in a sorority. Life-long friendships were made, and team members would never let each other down. The memories made of games lost and won, of victory parades and parties that were full of laughter and fun, and being prominent in the school yearbooks, year after year, would stay with her forever.

Her older brother, Vinnie, drove a beat-up Ford. When he enlisted in the service, she begged him to let her drive it when she got her driver's license. He not only agreed, but as a surprise for her, he had an arooga horn installed in it by Frank at the auto body shop. Oh, the fun she had driving her friends around after a Chargers win, honking the loud horn from one end of town to the other! *'Arooga! Arooga!'*

This was normally something a guy would do, but Geneva was totally comfortable behind the wheel with her foot on that button on the floor.

When the prom was coming up, she was asked by several young men to be their date. She turned them all down and, instead, invited a very shy boy, Bennett McHugh, who was relentlessly teased by his classmates because he was a big clumsy kid and had raging acne. He was shocked, but he said yes. On the evening of the prom, he looked quite handsome in his white tux, and Geneva saw to it that he had a wonderful time and taught him a few dance steps. He told her it was the best night of his whole life. Benny suddenly gained stature among his peers and confidence in himself, and the bullying stopped.

Geneva had a kind heart.

She entered nursing school after graduation, but fell in love with a young man, Matthew Hollis, the brother of a close friend. They married and had two children shortly thereafter. She had to put her dream of being a nurse on hold, and dedicated her young life to her children and her husband.

Sadly, as was the case far too often in those days, Matt lost his life in the war, and she was left to raise her son and daughter herself, with the help of her parents and her older sister, Rosalie. Eventually, she returned to nursing school and had a rewarding career as an R.N., retiring at sixty-six years of age, with a nice pension.

Now, at seventy-nine, she was still very attractive, spry, a little mischievous, and had lots of friends, many of whom had stayed close since high school. Her children were in their fifties and had families of their own. Their jobs had taken them out of state, but they managed to see her three or four times a year. The next time would be for the Festa Italiana in July.

La Festa

It was July 12th. The festival was coming up the following week, and when the brothers went for their haircuts, Ernest told Sal that he wanted to take Newell but he was concerned about the crowds and wanted to know if Sal could set up some chairs for them in front of the shop, which was right in the middle of the action. Sal said, "Sure! No problem! I'll set up two chairs and put your names on them, right in front so nobody takes them. It's a good time. Bring your appetitos!"

It was a three-day celebration, and they decided to go on the first day. Sal had mentioned that there was no parking in the area, so they took the bus, which let them off right behind the shop. Newell needed Ernest's assistance climbing the steep stairs of the bus, but this would have been absolutely impossible before his commitment to get stronger.

Sure enough, there were two folding chairs on the sidewalk in front of the window. Sal had put a sign on each one saying 'RESERVED' with their first names underneath. He had tethered the legs together with a small bungee cord.

The aromas emanating from the food stands were intoxicating: sausage and peppers, pizza, meatballs, arancini, ravioli, braciole, and grilled meats of all kinds. Everywhere you looked there was food. Before they sat down, they took a walk past the pushcarts, simply amazed at the selection of Italian specialties.

And the sweets! Fair-goers were either walking or seated at tables with red and white paper tablecloths, eating zeppole, a pillowy fried dough covered in powdered sugar, cannoli, gelato, and granita, which was fruit-flavored crushed ice in a paper cone. Even if you weren't hungry, you would be hungry.

There were hundreds of people milling about. Young and old, alike, were dancing in Trentino Square, across from the shop. The loud and lively music was coming from a foursome playing a guitar, an accordion, a mandolin, and a tambourine. A woman, wearing a white peasant dress with a wide red belt, sang Italian songs into a microphone, most of the tunes in a waltz rhythm. The dance-crowd was interspersed with couples dressed in traditional folk costumes: the men in black pants with white puffed long-sleeved shirts and colorful sashes around their waists, and the women in white ruffled blouses and flowered skirts, wearing white stockings, black patent-leather shoes, and lace handkerchiefs on their heads. It was a spirited and energetic scene.

A row of arcade games was busy, and a crowd of delighted children was watching an organ grinder cranking music out of a wooden box on wheels. He had a tiny Capuchin monkey in a costume doing cute tricks for pennies. A few blocks away, there was an area with a Ferris wheel, and several other carnival rides. Red, white, and green decorative lights were strung over the street, along with festive flags and balloons, and people had their dogs dressed in red, white, and green, too.

The brothers had never seen anything like it! The atmosphere was electric, and Newell could not stop smiling. There was just so much to see and hear and smell. It was an exhilarating spectacle to take in, a sensory explosion, and he loved it.

"This is just great!" he said to Ernest as they sat watching the masses of people stroll by. "Catherine and I used to love people watching. It doesn't get any better than this!"

"I'm going to get something to eat. What do you feel like?" Ernest asked, getting up.

"Those sausage and pepper sandwiches looked good to me. That's what I'll have," Newell said, reaching for his wallet.

"I'll get this one. You can get the next one," Ernest said with a smile and headed up the street toward the food vendors. Newell sat back, patted his thighs, and was pleased that his efforts on the pedal exerciser had paid off, allowing him the mobility to enjoy this day.

In the street, right in front of the barber shop, were three oak half-barrels, partially filled with big, purple grapes. Two women and a man with scarves around their necks were yelling to the crowd – "Come! Stomp some grapes! Grape stomping! Win a prize!"

Newell watched as, suddenly, three older women ran up to the barrels, giggling. They all kicked off their sandals and were helped into one barrel each by the three who had been soliciting business. Two of the women were wearing Bermuda shorts, and the one closest to Newell had a skirt on, which she clutched around her knees to keep it from being stained by grape juice.

At the count of three, "Uno! Due! Tre!" the women began to crush the grapes with their bare feet. They could not stop laughing, trying to keep their balance and not giving a hoot what they looked like. The one who got the most juice out of a spigot on the bottom of the barrel would be the winner. A crowd had gathered around them, and everyone was clapping, and yelling, "Vino! Vino! Vino!"

It lasted several minutes, and the women were exhausted from laughing and stomping the grapes. The woman farthest from Newell won, and they placed a wreath made of grapevines and small yellow silk flowers on her head. The ladies were helped out of the barrels by spotters who had held their hands to steady them, but the woman closest to Newell tripped on her skirt, lost her balance getting out, stumbled a few steps, and fell right into Newell's lap!

Most women would have been mortified, but she couldn't stop laughing. She turned to look at Newell's face and said, breathlessly, "Why, you look familiar! What year did you graduate?"

Newell was flabbergasted. Here he was, eighty-one years old, in the middle of hundreds of people, with a strange woman sitting on his lap.

She showed no signs of wanting to get up, so he answered her, and she said, "Oh, gosh, I used to be a cheerleader when you were playing for the Chargers! I had the biggest crush on you! I'm Geneva Conte! And you are Newell Madison! You probably didn't even know I was alive!"

He gently helped her off his lap and into Ernest's chair. One of her friends tossed her a towel and her sandals then disappeared into the crowd.

"You look wonderful, Geneva! I had a crush on you, too, but I thought you were way out of my league, so I never approached you. I didn't think I had a chance!"

"Well, you do *now*. Let's dance!" and she pulled him up from the chair and led him out into the square into the undulating crowd. She was barefoot, and her feet and legs were blue from the grapes, but she didn't care.

"I, I can't. I can't dance anymore," Newell muttered, as Geneva was putting his arm around her waist.

She placed her left hand on his shoulder, and grasped his left hand in her right. She was tall, and they made a good fit. "Oh, nonsense!" she said, and led him into a 'one-two-three' dance step.

He was dancing! He was laughing! They couldn't even talk because the crowd and the music were so loud, so they just grinned at each other, twirling around and around. One song was going to blend right into the next, but Newell shook his head indicating that he couldn't continue, so they walked back to the chairs holding hands, and sat down just as Ernest came along with the sandwiches.

"Well, well, well! Hello there!" Ernest said, looking from Newell to Geneva and back again.

"This is Geneva Conte. We went to school together, different grades. Geneva, this is my brother, Ernest," Newell said, trying to catch his breath.

She said, "Oh, it's Geneva *Hollis*. Nice to meet you, Ernest! Newell and I have just had a wonderful reunion! My children are visiting from out of state. They're here, somewhere! I guess they'll find me!"

Newell smiled weakly as he tried to hide his disappointment.

"Well, I'll let you two have your lunch. So wonderful to see you again, Newell! It's a three-day festival, you know?" She stood up, took both of his hands in hers, leaned down and kissed his cheek and said, "Ciao!" She winked at him, then hurried off to meet her friends who had been waiting for her across the square.

The brothers ate their delicious sandwiches, enjoying the sunshine and the festivities. Newell was the happiest he had been in a very long time, but at the same time, he felt a twinge of sadness because Geneva had given Ernest her married name. She had children…and a husband.

Then, Ernest said, "She seems really nice. I remember the Conte family. They were very well-liked in town. Sad that she lost her husband in that hellacious war. I'm really lucky that I came back alive and in one piece!"

Suddenly Newell perked up and said to Ernest, "I really enjoyed myself today! I felt *alive* for the first time in *years*. Any chance we could come back tomorrow?"

Ernest smiled. "Sure, why not? This was a good time! A nice change of pace. I'll just call Sal and ask him to save our seats again. He won't mind. And you can pay for the pizza!"

That night in bed, Newell's mind was racing, remembering the day:

the sights, the sounds, the smells, the EXPERIENCE.

He thought about his arm around Geneva's waist and dancing with her to the lively Italian waltz. He pictured looking into her laughing brown eyes and remembered the kiss, the wink, and her hint that she might be there tomorrow. Just as he nodded off to sleep, he thought to himself, smiling, *"Take it slow, Newell. We can do this."*

Epilogue

They were having lunch at Millie's. Ernest got his regular chicken salad on white, hold the pickle, and an Orange Crush. When Gracie asked Newell what he wanted, he startled her by saying, "Surprise me!" Gracie giggled, and in a couple of minutes, brought him a B.L.T., crusts intact. He gave her an appreciative grin and took a big bite, mayonnaise dripping down his chin.

"So…" Newell began, "I had this craving for fried chicken…"

And a real conversation began, sprinkled with an outburst of laughter here and there. Millie, Gracie, and all the regulars secretly watched in astonishment because they had never heard laughter from these two before, and they had all overheard their fair share of squabbles.

The brothers finished their meals and got up to leave, leaving Gracie a good tip, as always.

The brothers walked together down the three steps to the sidewalk and over to the Buick parked at the curb.

Ernest said, "You want to drive?"

Newell shouted, "Hell, no!" and they fell into the seats, laughing.

As Ernest pulled out into the street to head home, Newell said, "Make it snappy, brother. I have to squeeze in a nap this afternoon." With his wide, toothy grin, he said, "I have a date tonight."